Feline Heat

By

Madelaine Montague

Paranormal Romance

New Concepts   Georgia

Be sure to check out our website for the very best in fiction at fantastic prices!

When you visit our webpage, you can:
* Read excerpts of currently available books
* View cover art of upcoming books and current releases
* Find out more about the talented artists who capture the magic of the writer's imagination on the covers
* Order books from our backlist
* Find out the latest NCP and author news--including any upcoming book signings by your favorite NCP author
* Read author bios and reviews of our books
* Get NCP submission guidelines
* And so much more!

We offer a 20% discount on all new Trade Paperback releases ordered from our website!

Be sure to visit our webpage to find the best deals in e-books and paperbacks! To find out about our new releases as soon as they are available, please be sure to sign up for our newsletter (http://www.newconceptspublishing.com/newsletter.htm) or join our reader group (http://groups.yahoo.com/group/new_concepts_pub/join)!

The newsletter is available by double opt in only and our customer information is *never* shared!

Visit our webpage at:
www.newconceptspublishing.com

New Concepts Publishing, Inc.
5202 Humphreys Rd.
Lake Park, GA 31636

ISBN 978-1-60394-157-0
© Dec. 2007 Madelaine Montague
Cover art (c) copyright Dec. 2007 Eliza Black

NCP books are available at special quantity discounts for bulk purchases for sales promotions, premiums, fund raising, or educational use. For details, write, email, or phone New Concepts Publishing, Inc., 5202 Humphreys Rd., Lake Park, GA 31636; Ph. 229-257-0367, Fax 229-219-1097; orders@newconceptspublishing.com.

First NCP Trade Paperback Printing: February 2007

Chapter One

"You're up next, Kate! Move it!" Marty growled.

Kate's belly instantly knotted into a tight ball of fear. Her heart rate shot up and her lungs began to labor to drag in air. Breathe, Kate, she commanded herself! Deep breath in, exhale slowly. Deep breath in, exhale.

Her mind was chaotic. It was a wonder she even managed to gather enough sense to focus on breathing slowly to keep from hyperventilating.

The man airbrushing the last of her 'costume' on, hurried to finish at Marty's prompting and finally stepped back. "You're ready."

Like hell!

She didn't voice the thought aloud. In the months since she'd 'agreed' to dance for Panas to work off her ex's gambling debts she'd learned it was a lot safer just to smile and nod like a good little slave and jump to do what she was told. If she looked sullen or moved too slowly she was liable to get slapped stupid. Voicing a complaint was just an invitation to get the shit beat out of her.

To the Russian mob that ran the operation, the Exotique`, the 'weaker sex' just meant easier control and they weren't the least bit bashful about using their superior strength to exert it.

Her knees felt like the bones and cartilage had melted to the consistency of jelly as she stood up from the bench where the man had been applying her 'costume' and surveyed the results in the tiny mirror above her make-up table. Her hair, which she'd always worn fairly long, had grown nearly to her waist, she saw with a touch of surprise, but it still fell short of concealing her nakedness. It had been lightened from her natural medium to dark brown with auburn highlights to a shade of red she'd hated since the first time she looked at it.

She was a feline tonight. God only knew what breed of cat

she was supposed to be---Liger?---her skin was hyena with dark stripes here and there.

She decided she looked like a walking camo for a jungle setting rather than any kind of cat from the wild as she dropped weakly to the stool in front of her table and quickly darkened the tip of her nose, gripping her eyebrow pencil in a trembling hand to sketch a wobbly trio of 'whiskers' on either cheek.

She'd gotten used to standing bare assed naked on the stage in front of a roomful of hooting men—as used to it as she was ever going to get—but the special 'treat' the management had in mind for the night had threatened to turn her bowels to water.

She was supposed to 'make love' to her feline 'mates' on stage—an 'artistic' imitation of the act in dance, she'd been assured, not in actuality, but the 'props' weren't merely stuffed animals like those Panas typically used. He'd brought in two very much alive, great cats—drugged, he'd assure her, almost to the point of unconsciousness, chained, but still alive—and still dangerous because they were straight from the wild, not even close to tamed or trained beasts.

Of all the bizarre things that prick, Panas, had thought up, this one was light years ahead of anything else.

For the first time in her life, she wished *she* was drugged—too high to have any idea of what was going on.

They were bringing the beasts onto the stage when she arrived and positioned herself for the opening of her act. She thought for several horrifying moments that she was going to pee on herself, or worse, as she watched the keepers lead first an enormous Siberian Tiger and then an equally huge African Lion out on the stage and secure the chains threaded through their bejeweled collars to an eye bolt embedded in the floor on either side of the stage.

Both cats staggered drunkenly, their movements slow, awkward, as if they were swimming through water. It reassured her a little, gave rise to pity she hadn't anticipated.

The tiger dropped heavily onto his side once the three men half dragging, half pushing him managed to get him within reach of the bolt to secure his chain.

It also reassured her to see that they'd only left enough play in the chain to allow him to lay as he was. She doubted he'd be able to get to his feet.

He was absolutely enormous, though. She'd had no idea the things were so huge.

And muscled. She could see the muscles rippling beneath his beautiful coat.

As tall as the Russian thugs were, she'd be willing to bet he would top them by several feet if he stood on his hind legs.

A shot of knee weakening adrenaline spiked through her when she discovered the cat was watching her through narrowed golden eyes. As dulled as they were by the drugs pumped into him, she saw a gleam of both intelligence and interest in those golden depths as he surveyed her with unblinking intensity.

She hoped to hell they'd fed him before they brought him out!

Shivering, she dragged her gaze from the tiger and watched the men securing the lion. Like the tiger, he was a magnificent specimen. His coat sleek and healthy, his mane thick and luxuriant, he was nearly as big as the tiger. He was also almost as 'brawny'.

And, like the tiger, he seemed far more interested in her than he was in the men moving around him.

The men stepped off curtain, but they remained well within her view.

She wasn't reassured by the fact that they'd taken up the poles with loops on the ends she'd seen animal handlers use to catch and control animals.

Stinging prickles of dread rippled over her skin as she heard Panas, just on the other side of the curtain that still concealed her from the audience, trying to work the almost exclusively male audience into fever pitch anticipation.

The noise from the audience rose to a volume that literally vibrated the wood beneath her feet.

The cats stirred uneasily, dragging their focus from her to stare at the curtains, their ears flicking and turning on their uplifted heads like miniature radar tracking dishes.

She'd become the most popular dancer, a situation that

mystified her and caused her no end of trouble with the other exotic dancers. She had two breasts and a pussy—just like they did. She thought she had a pretty good figure, but it was by no means the best—certainly not when 'best' seemed to be measured in the size of the breasts. She was older than all of the others, most of whom were barely twenty while she was breathing hard on thirty. And she was absolutely certain she didn't dance better. In fact, despite the fact that she'd gotten used to it, more or less, and generally managed to focus on the music instead of the men leering and hooting at her, she was still too shy of flaunting her nakedness to really relax, definitely too inhibited to fan her legs and expose her 'tonsils' like the others so often did. It took all she could do to keep her arms and legs moving, at all, and refrain from covering herself.

She strongly suspected it was the very fact that she looked so ill at ease and refused to show anything she could keep from showing that drove them up the wall.

She was so caught up in her thoughts, the curtains had already begun to part before she realized the moment was upon her. It was the music that actually caught her attention, however.

Drums. Jungle drums.

Her heart paced itself to match the beats, thudding heavily with each pat on the deep bass drum than accentuated the rhythm being played out on the lighter drums. She lifted her arms, beginning to gyrate slowly as the curtains swung wide and the spot lights, thankfully, half blinded her, making it almost impossible for her to see beyond the edge of the stage.

A half dozen dark skinned men, dressed in African garb, sat cross legged with the drums they were beating between their legs, three on either side of the stage.

She wondered if any of them had any idea that they were sitting directly in front of a lion and a tiger.

She somehow doubted it. They looked way too relaxed and focused on the music they were making with their drums.

Dead silence fell over the crowd as they spotted the two beasts and discovered the cats were watching them. The certainty that their attention was focused more on the cats than her drained some of the tension and stiffness from Kate as she moved slowly forward on the stage until she was positioned directly between the two cats. She went through the motions of 'offering' herself, wondering if the sweat popping from her pores and beginning to coat her body was enough to wet the paint that had dried on her skin and if she was smearing her stripes as she ran her hands over herself, cupping her breasts and massaging them.

The moment she did, she discovered the cats certainly didn't have their undivided attention. The steady beat of the drums drowned out most of the comments so that they blurred into an incomprehensible mumble, but she heard enough 'yeah, baby!' and 'bring it on, mama!' to assure her she'd recaptured their attention. She gyrated around to one side so that those on either side of the audience could get a better look at her assets, tucking her chin as if she was gazing down at herself and cutting her eyes at the tiger.

She had his full attention, too, she discovered, feeling her heart leap. His gaze was slumberous, but riveted on her nevertheless. Her heart was in her throat as she danced a little closer to him and pretended she was trying to entice him, moving sinuously while she felt herself up.

He studied her movements with an unblinking stare for many moments before he lifted his head and met her gaze. She tensed as he did, unable to prevent herself from meeting that golden stare, even though she had a bad feeling it was the wrong thing to do. Tearing her gaze from his after a moment, she turned away from him and moved slowly closer to the lion. As if she was trying to make up her mind of which to choose between the two, she turned from the lion after a few moments and moved back toward the tiger, inching a little closer each time. She'd made the circuit twice when she discovered Panas the Prick watching her from the wings—glaring at her actually, and motioning imperiously with his hand toward the animals.

Their fucking paws weren't nailed to the floor, she reflected with a burst of anger fed by fear—drugged and chained, or not, they hadn't shifted more than a hair, but both cats seemed way too mesmerized by her for Kate's peace of mind. By the time she'd danced to first one cat and then the other again, the audience was shouting directions she didn't *want* to understand and Panas looked like he was going to burst a blood vessel.

She slithered down to her knees that time, more because it felt like her knees would give out than because she wanted to comply with Panas' demands.   Crawling toward the lion cautiously, she lifted a shaking hand and settled it on his side, hoping his reach wasn't long enough to knock her head off of her shoulders if he felt inclined to slap at her.

She felt a vibration filter through her palm as she stroked his fur from his belly to his hip. For several moments, her mind was so perfectly blank with terror, she couldn't figure out what the vibration was.

Then she realized he was purring.

It heartened her, but not by a hell of a lot.

Realizing her legs were too weak for her to actually regain her feet, she crawled across the stage to the other cat, approaching him warily. He tensed when she touched him and her heart tried to choke her. Almost as if he forced himself to relax, the muscles beneath her hand eased. She stroked her hand through his fur, feeling a rumbling purr begin from deep inside of him, but she couldn't work up the nerve to move closer.

She was supposed to rub herself on them.

She didn't think she could do that.

Trying to assure herself that Panas wouldn't beat her to death for deliberately ignoring his orders, she moved back to the lion and stroked him again. He began to purr again almost the moment she touched him, shifting almost restlessly, as if he wanted to turn to draw closer to her. Thankfully, the chain kept him from getting close enough to sniff her. She could see his nostrils flaring, though, knew he was 'tasting' the air for her scent.

Panas was making motions with his hands again when she dared a glance in his direction.

As she moved back to the tiger once more, the tiger watched her every move. The moment she reached out to begin stroking his belly and hip again, however, he lay down completely, settling his head against the floor and stretching his great body out as if inviting her to rub his belly.

Slightly reassured by the fact that his head, and those frightening jaws, weren't hovering over her, she inched a little closer and rubbed her face along his belly.

As quick as lightening, he hooked one great foreleg around her shoulders and dragged her full length against his belly. Before she could even remember her voice to scream, his huge head settled next to hers and she heard a rumbling, threatening growl directly in her ear.

* * * *

Sergei struggled against the effects of the drugs in his system, even though he'd learned by now that the fight was useless—worse than useless, actually. They'd brought him down with the drugs. When he'd wakened in a cage, he'd loosed his fury on the people who'd captured him, battering at the bars that imprisoned him until they'd raced to get more of the drug and used it to take his will to fight. He hadn't been lucid enough since that time to manage much more than eyeing them with deadly promise every time they came near his cage to feed him or drug him again.

He knew, though, that he was far, far from his home. Despite the drugs, he'd been aware of the passage of time in the elevation of the stench around him, the number of times he was fed and hosed down to cleanse the offal from his cage, which was barely big enough for him to turn around in much less to distance himself from his own excrement. The incessant heaving and rocking beneath him that made him too sick to attempt to fight even if not for the drugs had finally translated in his mind to 'ship' even though he'd never been on one before—had not traveled in any of the machines of man since he'd eschewed that side of his nature in favor of the wilds when he'd finally realized it was safer, both for him and for the man-children, for him to stay as far away from them as possible.

He was not of their kind, even though he had walked among them during much of his early years, nor yet of the beasts that was his other side. In truth, he belonged no where, but he preferred the honest savagery of his beast kindred to the brutal lies and deceptive nature of the man-children.

At least the beasts he lived among only killed for survival—to eat, to protect, for self-preservation—never merely for amusement or vindictiveness. They would not hunt him down and kill him only because he was different as they had his parents because they had been foolish enough to believe they could pass undetected among the man-children.

It had settled in his mind after a time that, if they hadn't killed him outright, they had a reason for allowing him to live. They had plans for him and that meant he still had the chance to live. All he had to do was bide his time. Sooner or later they'd slip up, become too confident, and when they did, they would pay for it with their lives and he would be free again, free to return to his life—such as it was.

The hunger to find another of his kind had eaten at him for years, the need for companionship, the need to mate. It had gone unfulfilled. In his beast form, he'd ranged far and wide and never sensed the presence of another like himself at all, let alone a female of his kind.

It was the need that had finally driven him back to the villages of man-children to walk among them, the hope that he'd find another of his kind there, living among them as he and his parents once had, but that hope had not only soured, it had gotten him captured.

He could only bear the constraints of his human skin for short periods before the itch to roam the wilds became nearly unbearable and it was his proximity to the man-children that had caught the notice of the hunters, he knew.

The irony was that those who'd captured him had brought him closer to another of his kind than he'd been since the deaths of his parents.

The South African was closer than he'd come before, at any rate. He was man-beast. He was feline—unfortunately not tiger, but it had given rise to renewed hope that he might know where others of their kind were.

He would find out when he found a way to free himself—for they had no way to communicate when they did not dare take their human forms—and if the lion knew of others, maybe he'd help him escape, as well.

And if he did not—maybe he would anyway.

He'd curbed his fury after a while, once it had finally settled in his thick skull that fighting them was not only useless, it encouraged them to keep him too drugged to use his wits. They still gave him far too much to have much mind about him, but at least he was awake part of the time now. At least he could see what was going on around him. At least his rambling thoughts connected from time to time.

As they had when he'd been brought to this place.

He was to be sold to a zoo, he'd discovered, but they hadn't found a buyer yet. They'd decided to make him 'earn his keep' by entertaining in their club/casino.

The first discovery had increased his rage to the point where he'd had difficulty pretending he was still too drugged to hold his head up, let alone alert enough to try to fight them.

The second discovery had made him glad he'd managed to contain his fury.

They were going to take him out of his cage.

When they did, he would have his first real opportunity to escape—if he was lucky.

He'd underestimated their wariness of him. Despite the fact that he'd pretended to be more than half asleep, they'd taken no chances. They'd shot him up with more of the hated drugs, waiting until they were certain the drugs were pumping through him before they'd opened the cage.

He'd tried to gather himself to launch an attack anyway, but had discovered he could barely stand. Reality had blurred around him as they fixed the collar around his neck and half dragged him from the cage, poking and prodding him until he'd stumbled to his feet. He'd had to splay his legs wide to remain standing once he'd gotten up and the drug had skewed his perceptions, making it almost impossible to walk. It had required absolute concentration to put one foot in front of the other and move when they'd started dragging on the chain and choking him with the collar around his neck.

Impotent rage had risen to life inside of him, but deeply, too deeply to summon it to his aid.

And then he'd seen *her*.

From the moment he'd spied her his entire focus had shifted to her. A hunger he barely recognized rose instantly and began gnawing at his gut, flooded his already drugged mind with a drug far more potent. He'd thought she wasn't real at first, tried to shake the image, tried to convince himself he was seeing things, and then he'd caught her scent and that had only confused him more. The drugs, he wondered? She looked like a she-beast, but she smelled human. Was she both, as he was? Or only human?

He struggled to recall the scents of his parents, to remember if they carried the smell of both man and beast, but he couldn't seem to remember. It seemed possible, though, that she would have the scent of man-child when she was in half-shift.

He didn't know, but he discovered he didn't care. Hunger pervaded him as he stared at her. Need surged through his body, setting it on fire. His man side wanted her with a feverish need that had him fairly quivering with the restraint he had to struggle to hold on to. His beast side decided he would have her.

The lion-man, he realized fairly quickly, wanted her, too. He could see the hunger in the other beast-man's eyes—smell it on him.

Savage possessiveness moved through him. He wanted her and he *would* have her. If he had to tear the lion-man's throat out and crawl over his bloody carcass to get her, he would!

She made it easy for him. After teasing him until it was all he could do to remain perfectly still and wait for his chance, driving him more mindless by the moment with the promise of her undulating body, her scent, and tentative touch, she made the mistake of moving within his reach.

He caught her, dragging her close enough he could finally wallow in her scent, immerse himself in it, the scent that had been driving him steadily closer and closer to madness. He could feel the warmth and softness of her and the instant he did, he lost his hold on his last tenuous thread of reason.

Chapter Two

The instant she shifted onto her knees, Sergei pounced, driving his cock into the warm cavern of her womanhood, and the moment he felt her tight flesh close around his length, a euphoric cloud of ecstasy rose in his mind. He could no more have stopped the primal urge to pound into her until he lost his seed than he could've stopped his own heart.

He needed this, *needed* it. She was made for him, he thought dimly, feeling a savage joy flood him as her hot flesh surrounded his, fisted around his cock so tightly he felt like his heart would explode.

She wanted it—wanted him. She'd chosen him. Despite the fear he'd smelled emanating from her, she'd come to him, rubbed her scent all over him, positioned her body to entice him.

* * * *

Shock swallowed Kate so completely within its maws that her entire consciousness narrowed to one tiny point—she was aware of the heat and weight of his body, the tight, unrelenting hold he had on her, and nothing else. Terror clawed at the back of her mind but couldn't break free to lend her a jolt of adrenaline to give her strength or unleash her instincts for survival. The rumbling near her ear deafened her to everything outside the hot cocoon that enveloped her.

Purring, a rumbling, intermittent purring emerged from his throat with each exhalation of breath, she realized dimly.

She got her knees under her and discovered it was the worst mistake of her life, the worst thing she could possibly have done at that moment.

Another wave of shock rolled over her as she felt him penetrate her. Time stopped. Her heart seemed to stop. Her lungs froze in her chest as an impossibly thick, hard shaft of flesh drove unrelentingly inside of her, sinking so deeply it pushed what little air remained in her lungs from her in a grunt.

A rash of goosebumps erupted all over her at the burning pain of his entry, of her flesh yielding to a greater force.

She sucked in her breath on a choked sob as he withdrew and plunged inside of her again, driving into her so frenziedly that her mind shifted to focus on that one point, the point of entry, and her body, with a will of its own, perhaps only in self-defense to prevent her flesh from tearing, sent a rush of moisture to ease his possession.

She might have told herself that later, might have soothed her horror that her body had no conscience, if it had been only that. Her body *also* had no mind of its own, though, and the shock had shifted the mind that should have exerted control over it out of gear.

Pleasure stirred to life the moment the pain eased. The thickness and length of his shaft left no nerve bereft of stimulation and the pounding beat of his rhythm no time to fight the rise even if she could've gathered her wits. Before her sluggish brain had managed to assimilate what was happening, her body began to quake and shudder with an explosion of such pleasure that it drove choked cries from her.

Darkness swarmed around her in the aftermath, freeing her from her shock even as she felt his legs tremble as he withdrew his shaft from her at last. Sucking in a harsh breath, she scurried away from him as she felt his grip on her ease, rolling once she'd pulled herself free and then scrambling to her feet.

The curtains, she realized dimly, had been drawn—sometime during the attack.

Panas and his goons were still frozen—hadn't moved so much as a hair that she could see.

Her brain gathered that information only in passing, however. When she'd managed to get her feet under her, she dashed from the stage in a blind panic to escape. As she fled through the dressing room, headed for the showers, her mind clicked like the shutter of a camera, collecting stills of the women staring at her in blank faced shock as she ran past.

She was shaking all over by the time she'd locked herself in the bathroom. She didn't wait for the water to warm up. Turning both knobs wide open, she leapt into the shower. The shock of the cold water snatched her breath from her chest, but it broke the grip of panic, as well.

Her teeth were chattering by the time the water warmed up.

The Siberian Tiger had humped her, she thought blankly!

No, *fucked* her!

She covered her face with her hands. Of all the things that had run through her mind when she'd discovered she was supposed to dance around two huge, dangerous felines, getting fucked by one of them *wasn't* it! Eaten, yes. Mauled, probably—not fucked.

The thoughts had no more than entered her mind than she dropped her hands and examined herself.

She didn't have a scratch on her!

Dumbfounded, wondering if the warmth of the water combined with the body paint, which still coated her skin, was preventing her from seeing or feeling scratches, she rubbed at her skin and finally grabbed the soap and scrubbed herself thoroughly.

There were tears around her sex from the size of the cock she'd had shoved into her—without warning—without time for the natural moisture of her body to ease its passage.

Considering the size of the thing, there might have been tears anyway.

She'd discovered the breaks from the sting of the soap, though. Thankfully, there was no blood. Her sex was throbbing like a son-of-a-bitch from the thorough pounding, but not damaged that she could tell.

She wasn't going to have to rush to the hospital and get sewn up.

A hysterical half giggle, half sob escaped her at that thought.

She thought she'd rather bleed to death than have to tell a doctor what had happened. No way was anyone going to believe she'd *accidentally* gotten fucked by a Siberian Tiger.

She slid down to the floor of the shower, curled into a tight ball, and just sat beneath the pounding water, dry eyed, trying to come to grips with how she felt about what had happened.

She realized after a while that all she really felt was relief— stunned disbelief that he'd grabbed her and she was still alive—without a scratch on her, in fact—embarrassment, for being   screwed—publicly—by   a   tiger—and   both embarrassment and shame that she'd come.

She'd been fucked by a tiger and she'd come!

She couldn't even remember the last time she'd had sex with a *man* and come!

Mentally, she beat herself up over it for a little while. About the time the hot water ran out, it occurred to her that she certainly hadn't *wanted* to. She hadn't sought it. She wasn't a pervert. It had just happened, and it had happened because stimulation was stimulation. Her body didn't know the difference and her mind had been out of gear at the time—too blown away by what was happening to have any control over her body.

It was Panas' fault, the fucking prick, she thought angrily, realizing abruptly that him and his men hadn't done a damned thing but watch. Not one of them had moved in to try to stop it.

If the tiger had decided to eat her when he was done fucking the hell out of her, he could've done it.

She still couldn't figure out why he'd wanted to 'romance' her in the first place.

Ok, so dogs humped anything they could latch on to. She didn't know about great cats. Maybe they were just as fuck happy?

Between the drugs they'd pumped into him and the body paint they'd used to make her look like a cat, the poor thing had probably *thought* he'd gotten hold of another cat.

She discovered when she finally decided to get up that she was bruised and sore. Every muscle in her body seemed to protest.

When all was said and done, though, considering her experience, she was in fabulous shape—head, arms, hands, legs, fingers, and toes all still attached. No gaping wounds with guts hanging out—no scratches even.

Her pussy felt the big scary pussy's presence but she thought, once she got over feeling like someone had fucked her with a fence post, she was going to be ok.

Someone was pounding on the door and on the verge of breaking it down by the time she got out of the shower. Someone had been pounding on the door almost from the time she'd leapt into the shower. She'd ignored it. She realized the fist currently beating on the door, though, belonged to either Panas, or one of his goons. The women screaming at her from the other side hadn't been able to shake the whole door frame.

He broke the door in before she could get to it and she saw it was one of Panas' goons. After surveying her thoroughly from head to foot, he stepped back out of the way and Panas sailed into the room. Grabbing her arm, he jerked her around and looked her over.

She didn't make the mistake of thinking it was actually concern.

He was frowning when he stepped back.

She didn't like the thoughts she could see flickering through his mind.

"It is good ting you are not injured," he said finally.

Anger surged through her. No thanks to him, she thought furiously. She swallowed the anger with an effort, tamped the urge to strike out at him for being entirely responsible for the incident and not protecting her when the cat had pounced on her. He wasn't pissed, but that didn't mean he'd take any lip off of her. The moment she opened her mouth to give him a piece of her mind, she'd be picking herself up off the floor.

Oddly enough, as soon as she'd regained control of her temper, she thought about the tiger and the possible consequences, to him, of what he'd done. "What are you going to do with the tiger?" she asked hesitantly.

His shaggy brows rose. He shrugged elaborately. "Nothing. Get dressed. You go home and rest for tomorrow."

Grabbing one of the paper thin towels provided by the management for the 'girls' usage after Panas and his goons left, Kate dried herself the best she could and wrapped the wet towel around herself. She felt the gaze of every woman in the cramped dressing room boring into her as she went to her locker to drag out her street clothes. Several snickers erupted as she stepped into her panties and pulled them up.

"How'd it feel to get fucked by a tiger?"

Kate felt her face redden. Hoping they wouldn't notice if she didn't turn around, she reached instead for her bra. "He humped me," she lied. "Don't get too worked up about it."

"That ain't what I heard," cooed another voice. "The guys

were all excited about it—said he fucked the hell out of you."

A shiver skated down Kate's spine. It wasn't hard to identify at least a part of the cause.

The 'girls' weren't the only ones titillated about the attack.

The men had been excited, and that probably included those in the audience, too. That was what that gleam was in Panas' eyes—dollar signs, she realized, feeling a wave of nausea wash over her. He was probably already counting the money people would pay to watch a woman get fucked by a tiger.

It didn't take much for her imagination to supply her with a vivid picture of it.

The second shiver that skated through her wasn't one she was willing to identify.

Ignoring the spiteful speculation behind her, Kate focused on dressing, trying to figure out what, if anything, she could do to prevent herself from becoming a part of the woman vs tiger act she knew Panas was currently putting together in his mind.

* * * *

Sergei's bliss over his woman lasted right up until the moment she slipped from his grip and took off. Instinctively, he tried to surge to his feet to give chase. The collar around his neck was an instant, brutal reminder of his current circumstances. He fell down as he reached the end of his tether, but scrambled to his feet again. Ignoring the fact that the collar was choking off his air, he surged against it anyway, trying to break loose in his determination to get to her before she could escape him completely. Finally, his knees wobbled and he collapsed from lack of air, rolling onto the floor and gasping for breath.

The sting of a needle caused a new reality to descend upon him.

He'd been so enthralled by the woman he'd completely forgotten the need to behave himself if he wanted to avoid being drugged again.

Rage flickered to life briefly, but he felt the effects of the drug dragging him down toward oblivion within moments and discovered it was all he could do just to keep his eyes open.

The lion-man, no doubt enraged that Sergei had come out the winner in their contest to see which of them got hold of the female, roared and charged against his chain, trying to get to Sergei until he got a dose of the 'happy juice', as well. Sergei smiled a loopy self-satisfied feline smile at the bastard as they led him away. Maybe he was going back into the damned cage, but he'd gotten the woman, by damned! His chest swelled with pleasure.

Mine, he snarled at the lion-man as he passed him.

Not that he was worried about it. He'd marked her, rubbed his scent all over her while he'd plowed into that delectably tight little hole of hers. He'd smelled her pleasure in the taking, heard her faint groans, felt her body shatter just as his had.

She *knew* she was his.

He was almost content as he settled in his cage again, felt only a faint flicker of anger when he heard the door slammed shut. Her scent still lingered on him, in his nostrils. He could smell her sex on his.

He also picked up the faint tang of blood and for the first time doubt shook him, guilt tugged at him.

He stared down at the faint smears on his cock in consternation, trying to bring enough order to his floating brain to figure out what had happened, why the blood was there. Her time, he wondered dizzily? No, he decided, it didn't have that scent to it. It was fresh blood, from a fresh wound.

He'd hurt her, he realized in dismay.

And that was when it abruptly dawned on him that he'd still been in beast form when he'd taken her. Feeling a coldness wash through him, he bent his head to sniff for any other signs of blood, trying to remember exactly what he'd done. All he could remember, though, was the mindless frenzy to have her that had washed over him when she'd lifted her hips for him.

He'd thought she was offering herself.

What the hell had he done?

* * * *

Kate had no real awareness of what it was that was floating in the back of her mind while she dallied, waiting for the other dancers to be on their way. On a conscious level, it was nothing more than a great reluctance to leave with them. They'd enjoyed her humiliation way too much. She didn't want to risk being accosted in the parking lot by a group of them and enduring more.

It was going to be hell working with them now, she thought, not that it had been smooth sailing before. They'd made fun of her when Panas had first dragged her in to work for him because she was older than they were. And she'd given them plenty to laugh about when she'd been learning the ropes. She'd tried her best to hide the fact that she was miserably uncomfortable about having to walk around naked, or the next thing to naked, all of the time, but with indifferent success. That insecurity had also made her awkward at dancing, although, ordinarily, she loved to dance and thought she was fairly good at it.

They'd hated her worse when the crowd had decided they liked her.

She didn't particularly care that they didn't like her—she didn't like them, but there was no getting around the fact that their antipathy made a rotten job even harder to bear.

Now that they had something new to jeer at her about it was going to be even rougher for a while.

Maybe a long while if Panas was thinking what she was afraid he was thinking.

She hoped she was wrong, but she knew in her gut she wasn't. The club was sleazy to start with because Panas was the king of sleaze. If he thought the incident had been well received by the audience, he wasn't going to have any qualms at all about making her repeat the 'performance' until everybody got tired of it.

Or the tiger got tired of fucking her and decided to eat her.

One of the two.

As the last of the dancers finally left, Kate grabbed her purse and headed out of the dressing room. Glancing both ways down the hall, she turned in the opposite direction from the way that led out, heading toward the large storeroom at the back of the club where the loading docks were. The cats were huge and she doubted they would've moved them far after the men had unloaded their cages.

She discovered her hunch was right as soon as she slipped into the store room. Two of Panas' goons were entertaining themselves with poking at the cats with the control poles. The moment she stepped into the room, she heard the low, threatening growls of the cats.

The bastards, she thought angrily. It wasn't bad enough the poor cats were in cages barely big enough to turn around in? It wasn't bad enough they had them drugged until they hardly knew which end was up? They had to worry the living shit out of them besides?

She glared at the men impotently, knowing there was nothing she could do. They were as mean as Panas and just as likely to slap her head off if she mouthed off at them.

It made her feel sick to her stomach to watch them. For several moments she wavered, trying to decide whether to stick around and hope they got called away so that she'd get the chance to see the cats, or to just leave.

She wasn't supposed to be in the back. If she just brazenly walked up to them and told them she'd come to see the cats, would they let her? Order her out? Decide she'd come to flirt with them and rape her?

The last wasn't nearly unlikely enough to suit her. The whole bunch of them were mean brutes and behaved as if they were perfectly welcome to knock any of the dancers down and have a go at them if the notion struck them. Some of the women actually didn't seem to mind.

She minded, though. She hadn't been able to work for Panas and come out unscathed, but she limited her contact with the men as much as possible and had managed to avoid their brand of 'foreplay' for the most part since her first few weeks.

She found she didn't want to just leave, though. She wanted to see the cats.

Specifically, the tiger. She didn't know why it seemed important enough to risk running afoul of two of Panas' goons, but it was.

After a few moments, she made her way carefully around the room and found a spot to watch, knowing sooner or later Panas would call upon them to help with clean up or restocking the booze.

As the minutes ticked by, though, she began to realize that the longer she stayed the more trouble she was going to be in if she was caught. She'd just decided to leave when the call she'd been hoping for squawked over the walkie-talkies. Dropping the poles, they picked up the talkies and spoke Russian into them—which she, unfortunately, didn't understand. They moved to grab a couple of crates of booze, though, and left. As soon as they'd moved far enough away she thought they wouldn't notice her, she began to ease toward the cages.

Both cats were looking right at her when she finally stepped from behind a stack of crates and directly into their view, their heads lifted with far more alertness than she'd expected. She studied them warily for a moment and finally moved a little closer.

They were wild, she reminded herself—straight out the wild.

She'd heard the men discussing the cats before they'd brought them in to the club—capturing and selling protected species was just one more of their many and varied enterprises. They trafficked in anything that would turn a buck.

Not that she knew that these two particular breeds were protected or endangered. She just knew that the Russian mob didn't know or care. They didn't care anything about *human* life. They sure as hell weren't going to worry about wild life.

As she studied the cats, she realized why she'd come, why she'd risked being caught. She had to know just how dangerous they were, because she knew her life depended on it. She was pretty sure what she'd witnessed when she'd come in was the answer she'd been looking for, too.

They were wild, and beyond that, from what she'd seen, they were being systematically tortured and tormented. If they remained pinned up like this for long, they were going to be insane, not just wild.

She sat down on a crate nearby—not close enough for them to reach her, but still close enough she could study them.

Even caged, they made her pulse beat erratically. They were beautiful, but deadly. Their size alone was downright scary. They could've been half as big and still been extremely dangerous. She hadn't wanted to go on stage with them the first time. If she hadn't been more afraid of Panas, at that time, than them, she wouldn't have. She sure as hell wouldn't have if she'd known what would happen.

When all was said and done, though, it could have been a hell of a lot worse than it had been.

It was *liable* to be much worse the next time.

She discovered when she emerged from her thoughts that they had settled in their cages and were studying her with two pairs of eerily intelligent golden eyes.

A shiver tickled its way up her spine.

* * * *

Sergei felt his heart quicken as the tantalizing scent of *her* drifted to him. Lifting his head, he listened intently to the faint sounds of movement that told of her approach and he still felt a jolt run through him as she stepped into view, her wide eyes full of wariness.

The guilt instantly resurrected itself, but he saw no reproach in her eyes as she stared at him. He wasn't certain what he did see, but not anger, not accusation. Thankfully, not even the revulsion he'd feared he would see.

He dragged his gaze from hers after a moment, allowed it to flicker over her in search of any signs that he'd hurt her. Relief eased the knotted discomfort in his belly when he saw no outward sign of injury.

There was no doubt in his mind, unfortunately, that he'd hurt her, but at least he knew the damage had not been life threatening. At least he could comfort himself with that—and the fact that she didn't seem to be emotionally traumatized.

There was no sign, now, of the she-beast about her. She looked purely man-child.

He realized with a sinking sensation in the pit of his belly that that was because that was what she was—*all* that she was—man-child. A sense of betrayal stung him, aroused resentment to join the indigestible knot of guilt and shame churning in his belly. He wasn't certain who or what he blamed more—his senses that had failed him, the drugs that had dulled them—or her.

He realized he wanted to blame her, though.

It was easier to blame her for the simmering rage he felt beginning to churn inside of him, fed by the guilt, the disappointment, the wounded pride he felt in discovering he'd fallen for the deception. Because he couldn't even comfort himself with the belief that he could blame it all on the drugs.

Lust had been his downfall. The moment he'd set eyes on her he'd wanted her. He'd lost any ability to reason. His beast had completely submerged his man mind. His instincts, his *need* for a mate had consumed him and he was afraid that would've been the case even if not for the drugs.

Why, he wondered angrily, had she come to stare at him in his cage?

To gloat? To assure herself that the stupid, dangerous, beast that had dared to touch her was caged and tormented as he deserved?

* * * *

Silvair struggled with the residual effects of the mind dulling drugs in his system, discovering they only made it easier for the desire burning in his blood to overwhelm him, opened him wide to the fury he felt that the tiger-man had taken the woman he'd wanted for himself.

It defied reason. He knew that on one level. He was no more inclined to desire a man-child to mate than a lioness—had never considered it before—and for the same reason. Neither was as he was and an actual mating was unlikely.

Unfortunately, it was his mating instincts that had been aroused—not purely lust, not something he could appease by expending himself on her a few times and dismiss.

He just didn't know *why* that need to possess had ensnared him.

The why of it didn't matter, he finally realized. It was there, had been from the moment he'd first seen her, and its hold on him was gaining strength, not dissipating as he'd hoped. He had to deal with it.

She was going to have to deal with it.

Chapter Three

Kate thought the first night she performed with the two great cats was the most frightening she'd ever experienced, but she discovered the second was worse. Her fear of the cats had overshadowed her fear of Panas enough that she'd balked at having to perform with them again—briefly. He'd slapped her hard enough she'd seen stars and then had spent the hour awaiting her turn to perform with an ice pack on her cheek to reduce the swelling.

And she'd still been so scared when the curtains went up that it was all she could do to move at all, much less with any fluidity to her movements. The cats, she could see, were drugged as they had been the night before, and yet from the moment she'd taken her position, neither one had taken his eyes off of her.

She had the feeling—*knew*—they were just waiting for her to get close enough to grab her. They surprised her. Although, at Panas' prompting off stage, she'd nerved herself to rub all over both of them, both cats had merely stared at her through sleepy eyes.

The lion had yawned.

Any doubts she'd had that Panas had wanted, indeed *expected*, at least one of the cats to pounce on her and fuck her silly, was banished when he barreled out the moment the curtains closed and began bellowing at her and his goons, accusing them of giving the cats too heavy a dose of tranqs, accusing her of slipping something to them. Stalking over to the lion, he kicked the beast in the belly. The lion uttered a low, threatening growl, but made no attempt to protect himself.

Unsatisfied with that reaction, he returned to Kate and knocked her down.

The moment he swung at her, however, both cats surged to their feet, charged to the end of their chains, and snarled, and swatted at him. Panas had bolted to the edge of the stage before he realized the chains were holding. Emboldened by the fact that they couldn't get to him, further enraged by their attempted attack and what it had cost him in his dignity, he stalked over to one of his men and snatched the pole from his grip. Kate had recovered enough to push herself up to a sitting position. Holding her face, she looked around for Panas just in time to see him swing the pole at the tiger.

He hit the beast twice on the hip and back before the tiger, ears flattened, teeth bared, lunged at him, making him jump back.

"Don't!" Kate gasped. "They don't understand!"

"They *will* understand!" Panas raged and then turned on her again. Stalking over to her, he grabbed a handful of her hair and dragged her to her feet, gritting his teeth in her face. "And *you* will understand! You will do exactly as you are told or you will live to regret it, bitch! They *paid* to see you fuck the beasts, and you'll get them to fuck you, tomorrow, or you'll be sorry and they will be very, very sorry!"

* * * *

In some part of her mind, Kate knew she wasn't thinking rationally, but from the moment the idea had sprang into her mind, she hadn't been able to shake it, had clung to it and repeated it over and over in her mind like a protective mantra.

She had to let the cats go. It was the only way. Panas was going to kill her, or get her killed—or kill the cats—if she didn't. *She* couldn't get away from him. She'd tried it once, right after he'd 'hired' her. She'd just packed her bags one night and took off, and when his men had found her and dragged her back, he'd convinced her not to try it again.

She didn't think beyond that 'simple' solution that had occurred to her as she crept back to the store room where the cats were kept. She wouldn't *allow* herself to think past that point. It was a solution. She needed a solution.

She had to wait so long, this time, before the men were called away, that she'd begun to have second thoughts. When they left, though, she promptly dismissed the attempts of logic to enter her brain.

The cats were sleeping. She paused for several moments, wondering if Panas' idiots had overdosed them on the tranqs. They seemed to be breathing alright, though, and she moved on, opening the rear walk-through door and propping it wide.

Rushing back to the cages then, she peered at the cats to make certain they hadn't roused while she was busy opening the door for their escape and then used the pry bar she'd picked up on her way in to pry the locks off of both cages. The moment she'd done so, she fled out the back way and raced around the building to her car.

She was tempted to stay long enough to see if the cats woke up and managed to get out before anyone discovered what she'd done, but she was too intent on getting home to establish her alibi for when they escaped. The hysteria that had been riding her from the time Panas had started slapping her around began to subside as she neared her home and as it did, rational thought began to flood into her mind in spite of all she could do to stem the flow.

She'd just released two man-eating felines, she realized in horror, into an environment neither one was familiar with, but also into one where there were unsuspecting people the cats might decide to feed on.

The club was in a rural area, true, miles from the city, but there could be any number of people in danger from what she'd done—stragglers leaving the club, country people living in the area. There was nothing to stop the cats from coming into town, for that matter.

She'd broken open the cages and propped the door open for them to leave. No way in hell was Panas going to believe it was anybody but her that had done it.

She didn't know what to do once all of that had descended upon her, but the fear that was uppermost in her mind was getting caught by Panas.

The cats had been asleep—so out of it with tranqs it dawned on her that they were probably *still* in their cages—no threat to anyone—except her.

The club looked quiet and dark when she reached it again but there were still cars in the lot. She recognized the one

Panas drove. Switching off her headlights, she drove into the lot and around the side of the building. Peering through the darkness toward the door, she finally decided it was still standing ajar.

That meant no one had discovered it yet.

She sat in the car, staring at the door, trying to decide what to do.

She'd broken the locks, she remembered. Maybe she could just stick them back on the cages and they'd think the cats had broken them trying to get out?

Maybe it would be better just to shut the door and leave?

Shut the cats up *inside* with Panas and his goons?

They had guns. They were at least as dangerous as the cats—the cats probably wouldn't stand a chance. She hadn't wanted anything to happen to them.

Finally, she decided to just sneak in and see if the cats had gotten out. If they were gone, she'd shut the door and then go home and call animal control. She knew they'd try to capture the animals alive.

It seemed the best possible solution to the mess she'd made.

She really, really didn't want to see if the cats were still inside, though.

What if they were out of their cages?

Rolling her window down a tiny crack, she listened to see if she heard anything—screams, growling, running feet.

The silence was really unnerving.

They'd probably woken up in this length of time and took off, she told herself.

She was still trying to decide what to do when two giant, half naked blond men came barreling out of the door, leapt the steps, and landed not two yards from where she sat in her car.

Her jaw dropped to half mast. The thought had only just clicked in her mind to shove the car in reverse and haul ass when a couple of Panas' goons staggered to the door, aimed the automatics they were holding, and began to pepper the parking lot with shots. Screaming, she jerked the car in reverse and stomped the gas. One of the blond giants grabbed the door handle on the passenger side of the car and snatched it open just as she hit the gas, diving in and landing half on top of her. The other took a flying leap and landed on the top of the car, almost caving the roof in. Screaming again, Kate slapped at the man who'd landed beside her with one hand, trying to beat him off and regain control of the wildly careening car with the other hand.

She didn't manage it.

Because it didn't occur to her to take her foot off of the gas.

She kept going, zigzagging wildly across the parking lot until she slammed into something that stopped the car, flinging her forward so that she slammed her head into the steering wheel and then backwards in the car seat. She was still dazed when the blond giant beside her ripped her seatbelt off, dragged her out of the car, hefted her onto one shoulder, and took off at a ground eating lope toward the woods surrounding the club.

The blood rushing to her head from the position added to the throbbing pain already blinding and disorienting her. Her face had never actually stopped hurting from Panas slapping her around, had merely lessened to a dull ache, and her forehead now throbbed from the contact with the steering wheel.

She'd been shot at. Due to her guilty knowledge of what she'd done, the first explanation that popped into her head was that they'd been shooting at her because they knew she was the one that had let the cats go. If she hadn't been sitting by the back door, watching, they might not have figured it out—at least not so quickly, but that had been a dead giveaway of her guilt.

They'd looked like they'd been in a fight, she recalled.

She wasn't certain how the two blond giants fit into that scenario, though.

They were complete strangers. She was certain she'd never seen them in the club before. Not that she'd gotten much of a look at them when they'd come charging out the door and leapt at her, but she would've remembered the hair. They both had long 'Tarzan' like hair—except blond—almost as long as hers, and both of those traits were very distinctive even if she hadn't gotten a good look at their faces.

One, the more 'petite' of the two, who didn't look like he was much more than six feet tall and somewhere between 200 and 250 pounds—hard to judge with all that muscle when she knew muscle weighed more than fat—which he didn't seem to have any of—had hair so pale it was closer to white than blond. If he hadn't been half naked, wearing nothing but a pair of jeans that made it clear just how lean and fit he was, she might have thought it *was* white. There was nothing else about him that said 'old', though, so the hair was definitely platinum blond, not white.

The 'big' guy was *really* big. The top of his head had barely cleared the top of the door and his shoulders were so broad she was almost surprised he hadn't gotten wedged in the door frame—six foot five, at least, and no less than 250 pounds, she was sure. His hair was more of a golden blond, but still distinctly blond, not brown.

Oddly enough, their skin was a golden brown—not pale like their hair—not European looking, but more like a pair of California's 'golden boys'. They didn't look like surfer dudes, but they also didn't look like Russians—maybe German? Scandinavian?

Panas' goons were monsters and these guys still stood out from the pack. She would've noticed if they'd ever been around even if not for the hair.

All of that aside, they'd been running from Panas' goons, she realized.

It didn't take a great leap after that to realize that the goons had been after the two men currently making off with her through the woods and they wouldn't have been after these two unless they'd done something Panas didn't like.

It didn't take much to displease Panas, but the most likely scenario that popped into her mind was that the two men had robbed Panas—and *she* had been waiting outside! He was going to believe she was in on it! Whatever it was they'd done, she looked like an accomplice because it looked like she'd been waiting outside for them and they'd taken her with them when they escaped.

They were dead. They were all dead, but she was probably

going to go first. If they didn't decide to kill her to lighten their burden to move faster, then Panas would when he caught up with her. And there was no doubt in her mind that he would. His reach was a long one and beyond him were the other Russian mobsters, a nationwide network of them—global wide, actually.

She had no idea how long they ran through the woods. She'd long since passed from being impressed with their stamina to just plain miserable before they finally stopped. The sky was already graying with approaching dawn when the man carrying her finally halted and allowed her to slide to the ground. Every part of her body was not only numb by then from poor circulation, the rush of blood to her head instantly made everything go black and the moment he eased his hold on her she sank to the ground.

The good news was that she was completely unconscious before she hit it and she didn't feel a thing.

When she regained consciousness, Kate discovered two men peering down at her through strange golden eyes—made more odd by the fact that they were so close to the same unusual color and the color didn't seem to go with the hair. They should've had blue eyes with hair like that.

Brothers?

Aside from the similar hair and eye color, though, their features weren't really that similar. There was a marked difference in every feature—eyes, nose, mouth, and even the shape of their faces. Both men, though, were handsome in the way of manly men—with harshly angular, well defined features that were purely male in appearance.

Nothing girlish pretty about either one aside from the long, beautiful blond hair.

Kate grunted inelegantly when she made an abortive attempt to sit up. Closing her eyes again, she felt around her head for something to explain why it felt like it would explode.

"Did you hit me?"

When neither one answered, she opened her eyes in time to see the two men exchange a glance.

"De udder man," the larger of the two answered.

Kate stared at him in dawning horror. She knew that accent. It had figured in her nightmares since Panas had taken over her life. "Russian?" she asked hoarsely, wondering if she'd fallen into the hands of a rival mob.

"Da. I am Sergei."

After staring at him for a long moment, she glanced at the other man. His face was grim. "Silvair," he responded in a clipped voice. "Vat you do vid dem men?"

Kate blinked at him. The only thing that filtered into her mind at first was that the accent was definitely different—not Russian. The name sounded French to her, but the accent didn't. "You're Russian, too?" she asked doubtfully.

"South African."

Kate blinked several times. "You sure are light skinned."

For a moment amusement gleamed in his eyes. "Unt you obviously doan know South African vas settled by de Dutch."

"Oh." That explained the Scandinavian look and the reason he sounded like an Arnold impersonator. It didn't explain the French name, but she supposed people weren't restricted to using names from their own culture.

The question that rose to mind, though, was why were these two—who sounded like they'd just gotten off the boat—together? Obviously, they couldn't be related as she'd thought they might be.

"You work for dis bad man, da?"

Kate swung her gaze to the first man, Sergei. The question was loaded, and she didn't have any trouble figuring out that working for Panas meant she was the 'enemy'. "Not because I *wanted* to," she said defensively. "He didn't give me a choice."

Again the two men exchanged a long, speaking look.

"We leave you, you tell dem where we go, da?"

Kate studied him uneasily. She didn't especially want to go with them—not when she knew Panas and his men would be after them. On the other hand, they'd be after her, too—because of them. Safer with them? Safer without them? "How could I tell them anything when I don't have a fucking clue of where we are?" she demanded testily. Her chin wobbled. "And I can't go back, anyway. They saw me leave with you. They'll think I had something to do with whatever you did and they'll kill me."

She could tell just from their expressions that they thought she needed killing if she was on Panas' payroll. She might've felt the same way in their place, but she was in the position of knowing there were a lot of people who worked for Panas who didn't want to.

"Vat good you be to us?" Silvair demanded. "You slow us down. Dey catch us. Ve know how to move fast and leave no trail. *You* vill leave a trail."

Contrary creature that she was, the moment they suggested they didn't want her along, she knew instantly that was the place to be—especially if it meant leaving her dead so she couldn't tell tales. "I know this area pretty well," she said hopefully.

"You say you haf no fucking clue where we are," Sergei pointed out.

Kate gaped at him in dismay. "Because we're in the woods."

"Da, and we travel in de woods."

Trying to ignore the sinking feeling in the pit of her stomach and the realization that she was bargaining for her life, Kate searched her mind for what she could do that might sound useful to them—at least until she could get away from them. The comment that 'she would tell' had bad vibes. It sounded like they meant to make certain she couldn't tell if they left her behind. "You two are foreigners, right? I'm sure I know a lot of things that would be helpful since you aren't from here."

Sergei dug in his jeans pocket and produced a wad of cash big enough to choke a horse. "Just need money, da? We haf money."

Kate stared at the money bug eyed. "You *robbed* Panas?" she asked, horrified, even though she'd suspected as much.

"Took," Sergei growled, as if there was any difference at all.

"He'll be after you—us. They'll think I helped."

"Not Panas," Sergei said with grim satisfaction that told its own tale and sent a shiver careening down Kate's spine.

She swallowed against the dryness in her mouth. If she'd had any doubt before that the two men were just as cold blooded, ruthless, and dangerous as Panas she no longer did. "Then whoever takes over his operation," she said hoarsely. "They'll want their money back, and they'll feel a need to make an example of you two for stealing from them."

Maybe she didn't actually want to be with these two after all?

"Vhy dey tink you help?" Silvair asked sharply.

Kate blinked at him. She had more trouble following his accent than Sergei's, thick as it was. She'd grown accustomed to the Russian accent. "I left the door open ... and I was outside the door when you came out with my headlights off. And you went with me when I left."

Silvair frowned. "Vhy you vas dere?"

Kate's color fluctuated several times while the reasons fluttered through her mind. "Uh ...," she said finally. "You didn't happen to see a Siberian tiger and an African lion while you were robbing the place? Because I let them go and if they weren't inside, then they're out here—with us."

Chapter Four

Again the two men exchanged a long look.

Confusion flickered through Kate.   Either there was something about that news they shared common knowledge of, or they had to know each other much better than she'd first suspected. People rarely did that unless it was with a person of like mine.

The fact that they appeared to be working together seemed to imply they knew each other well, of course, but she hadn't gotten that impression. They didn't just *sound* like foreigners because their working knowledge of English was barely adequate, there was some indefinable something about the two besides that that made them *seem* completely out of their element. And, if they hadn't been in the U.S. long, and they were from two countries so far apart, it seemed unlikely they would've known each before.

Nevada might be the gambling meca and always full of tourists from everywhere, but it wasn't exactly a place for ordinary people right off the boat—tycoons, yes, but no one who wasn't rich unless they were just addicted to gambling.

Wannabe gangsters?

Mentally, she shrugged. More like wannabe dead men if they didn't know better than to rob a mobster.

"*You* release de tiger and de lion?" Sergei asked in a 'let's get this straight' tone.

Kate reddened.   She didn't think she could adequately explain what had been going through her mind at the time. "I hadn't exactly thought it through," she said defensively. "Panas was making me … uh … perform with them and all I could think about was that, sooner or later, one of them was going to kill me. So I let them go."

Sergei flushed, feeling his face tighten with a mixture of discomfort and anger. *Perform*, he thought with rising ire?

He'd been seduced to perform for the audience?

He didn't look at Silvair.

He hadn't been completely lucid for a while, but he could remember 'performing' without any problem and he didn't doubt Silvair remembered it just as well.

He'd been more worried about hurting her afterward than he had been about the fact that he'd copulated with a human female—at all. In his defense, he'd been drugged. He was long past the maturity to mate and hadn't been within sniffing distance of a suitable female—and he'd been so out of it, he'd thought she was in half-shift.

It had taken a long time of sifting through his thoughts and impressions to finally arrive at the conclusion that he'd mistaken a human female for one of his own kind.

His body certainly hadn't objected.

He wondered uncomfortably if he would've been as mortified by his 'mistake' if he hadn't discovered he was performing to titillate the man-children?

It was hard to say which bothered him the most.

Kate frowned. "Does that mean you did or you didn't see them?" she asked uneasily. "I mean—if they got loose, they're dangerous. I have to call animal control about them before somebody gets killed."

Again Sergei and Silvair exchanged a look. This time, though, their expressions were grim. "Dey vill be tracking vid dogs," Silvair said, ignoring her question.

Sergei nodded, lifting his head and glancing around the area through narrowed, assessing eyes. "Dere is man-village near here?"

"There's a town," Kate responded a little doubtfully. "I don't know if it would be what you'd call a village—but we can't go there! Panas' men would be all over us!"

"Talk later. Ve need to move now before dey pick up de trail," Silvair said brusquely, rising to his full height abruptly.

Sergei nodded and rose, fixing her with a hard look. "You can keep up, you can come wid us. Slow us down, we leave."

That didn't sound nearly as bad as 'slow us down, we kill'. Kate nodded jerkily and struggled to get to her feet. "Where are we going?" she asked tentatively.

Both men ignored her, striking off toward the sun, which had just crested a peak of the mountain range lying before them. "My name's Kate, by the way."

The two men exchanged a glance. It was Sergei that turned to glare at her, though. "You talk too much, woman. Dey won't need to track. Dey will hear you."

Kate gaped at him for a moment before indignation arose. Glaring at his back as he turned away, she clamped her lips together and decided to ignore both men.

She had a headache anyway.

Truth be told, she hurt all over.

Some of the stiffness eased after about thirty minutes of walking, but by that time she had a worse headache, her feet were starting to hurt, she was hungry, and she had to pee.

She'd thought she was fairly physically fit right up until they started the trek through the mountainous forest. It had been a long night, though. By this time she would ordinarily have eaten and gone to bed.

She would've been asleep three or four hours, in point of fact.

The fear that had kept the adrenaline pumping through her system waned after about an hour and she realized she was about as thoroughly miserable as she'd ever been in her life.

She also remembered she'd left her purse in her car. There were two very bad things about that. The cops were bound to find it—and she didn't have two pennies to rub together, or any kind of identification, without the purse.

She dismissed the first nightmare fairly quickly. The cops were going to know who she was anyway, she realized, the minute they ran the registration.

The 'broke and no identification' was another matter. She slowed, turning to look back in the direction they'd come, wondering if she should go back. She really, really needed her purse. She couldn't go back to her place. What the hell was she going to do without money *or* identification?

A rustle in the brush nearby brought her mind instantly from the missing purse to the cats. Her flesh pebbled all over. She could almost feel the hair on the back of her head stand up. Wide eyed with terror, afraid to move any part of her body, she cut her eyes toward the brush. "Sergei?" she whispered in a quavering voice.

Her knees buckled when a ham sized hand clamped down on her shoulder. She managed to catch herself before she wilted all the way to the ground, but she got whip lash from jerking her head around to see what had gotten hold of her.

Sergei was frowning at her. "What?"

"I think one of the cats might be in the bushes over there," she whispered hoarsely, using her eyes to indicate the direction.

His frown deepened as he glanced at the brush. He sniffed. "Rodent. You afraid of de cats?"

Kate blinked at him. "Don't get me wrong—I love cats. But these are big fucking cats I'm talking about. Bigger than me. Bigger than …." She broke off and looked him up and down. "Well, maybe not bigger than you—but really big."

He looked disgusted. "You afraid of de cats, keep up."

"Yes, but …." She frowned as he turned and stalked off, but scurried to catch up. "I don't suppose either one of you has a gun?"

Both men stopped abruptly and turned to look at her with almost identical expressions of irritation. "Vhat ve do vid guns?" Silvair demanded.

Kate bit her lip. "Scare them off? I mean—I wouldn't want to hurt them, but what if they're following us?"

"Who?"

"The cats!" Kate snapped irritably.

Amusement flickered in Silvair's eyes. He glanced at Sergei. Sergei grasped her arm and lifted it, examining it. "Not enough meat," he pronounced, his own eyes gleaming now with amusement.

Kate was still gaping at him when he and Silvair turned and resumed their walk. "Very funny," she muttered. "You didn't see the way they were looking at me, though, with those creepy yell … ow…." She almost ran into them when they halted abruptly and turned to look at her. Glancing from one pair of golden eyes to the other, she reddened faintly. "They looked hungry. That's all I'm saying."

A jolt went through her when Silvair stepped closer, grasping a handful of the hair at the base of her skull and tugging it down to tip her face up to him. She was still gaping up at him in stunned surprise when he swooped down to cover her mouth with his, plunged his tongue within the sensitive cavity, and raked it boldly across hers. Another jolt went through her at contact. Confusion welled inside of her but before panic could gain a toehold, a tsunami of heat rolled over her. In the wake of it flowed a rash of pebbly skin that so sensitized her flesh that a shiver traveled all the way through her at the light brush of his skin every where it made contact with hers as he dragged her up against his body.

Her brain shifted focus from the hard chest her breasts flattened against, to the intoxicating flavor pouring through her from the stroke of his tongue along hers, to the hardness of the arms banded around her. And then lost all focus of anything beyond the pleasure bombarding it from so many directions at once that the effect was dizzying and completely disorienting.

Weakness had begun to filter through her quivering muscles by the time he lifted his mouth from hers. Fortunately, he didn't let her go completely or she would've wilted to the ground. It took an effort to lift her heavy eyelids and uncross her eyes when he lifted his head to stare down at her. "Sveet," he murmured huskily. "De lion like dis sveet meat, I tink."

Kate blinked at him as that comment slowly infiltrated her brain and it registered that he was amusing himself at her expense as Sergei had. Irritation sent a bolstering shot through her elasticized muscles just in time to support her as he released her.

Contrary to what she'd expected, Sergei wasn't grinning in appreciation of Silvair's humor when she glanced at him. He was studying Silvair angrily, his lips tight, his jaw clenched, his eyes glittering dangerously.

He growled something in his native tongue that sounded like a curse and stalked off. After studying her for several moments as if he was considering taking up where he had left off, Silvair, still looking pleased with himself, turned and followed.

Kate was irritated enough to consider, briefly, turning the other way and seeing if she could find her way back to her car, but only briefly. Reflecting that Panas' goons were probably scouring the forest for them even now and the lion and the tiger stalking the three of them, she hurried to catch up to the two comedians.

She was actually a little surprised Silvair had restrained himself as it slowly dawned on her that, in spite of the comment, he'd been just as affected by that kiss as she had been—well, maybe not *as* affected, but certainly not indifferent. Her dealings with Panas and his men had been a hard lesson in the European mentality where women were concerned. They were thugs to whom crime was a way of life. They didn't balk at murder and they certainly didn't worry their little heads about battery and rape. If they wanted, they took.

She would've liked to have been able to convince herself that Sergei and Silvair were of a different ilk—and she had to admit they certainly seemed a lot more easy going than Panas and his men—but they had that same 'untamed savage' air about them. The only reason she could figure that Silvair hadn't decided to throw her down in the dirt and fuck the daylights out of her was because he didn't think he could spare the time at the moment.

She hadn't actually figured that into the equation while she was trying to decide whether to follow them or run the other way. She supposed it had been hovering at the back of her mind. It always did these days. She'd almost forgotten, in fact, what it was like to be around men who actually gave a shit whether a woman was willing or not. It seemed so long ago since she'd lived in that kind of world that it was almost as if it had been someone else living it.

Maybe, she reflected, the life she'd been living had turned her mind? Her belly executed a little quiver of anticipation every time her mind recalled the forceful way he'd grabbed her and the sensations that had rolled through her when he'd kissed her. 'Not half bad' didn't begin to describe it. She couldn't remember the last time any man had had that kind of effect on her with no more than a kiss.

She also couldn't remember the last time she'd looked at a man, any man, and felt attracted—interested—wholly open to the idea of intimacy. The two men in front of her were stunningly attractive, better looking and built far better than any man she could remember meeting in her life, but she not only didn't think her mind should be running in that direction under present circumstances. She also didn't understand how it could when she'd stopped thinking of men, at all, in those terms.

Panas and his men weren't the only 'men in her life' that had given her a distaste for the male of the species. Those she'd been forced to strip and dance for hadn't given her any better opinion of them. The obscene gestures, comments, and animalistic sounds they flung at her as she performed for them disgusted her. It didn't make her feel sexy and desirable as it seemed to make the other dancers feel. It made her feel unclean.

It was almost as much a pleasure as it was a surprise to discover she could still feel a healthy interest in a male—even if it was two who were just as inappropriate as the thugs no doubt chasing them.

She didn't doubt, though, that they'd 'cure' her of her misplaced interest before this was over with.

* * * *

Silvair's irritation rose as his arousal slowly dwindled. He didn't exactly regret giving in to the impulse to kiss Kate. He'd been itching to get hold of her since the first moment he'd seen her and the fact that the tiger-man *had* gotten a taste of her had only increased the need to stake his own claim to her, not diminished it in any way. He wasn't exactly pleased, though, to discover that kissing her had only whetted his appetite for more—not now that he had enough of his wits about him to realize what she was.

Unlike the tiger-man, who seemed to think his desire for a human female was an unhealthy perversion—a fact that he would've found highly amusing if *he* wasn't focused on Kate—he saw nothing wrong with assuaging his needs on human females whenever the opportunity arose—which, granted, was damned rare—he was half human himself, after all. But he didn't have a 'taste' for them, had never considered that he did anyway. He used them if they were handy and willing and he had the itch, but he *preferred* women of his own tribe.

He would've liked to think that the illusion the humans had manufactured that she was she-beast lingered at the back of his mind even though he'd finally shed the effects of their damned drugs, but he couldn't comfort himself that it did any more than tiger-man was able to.

It was her—not the paint. He just wasn't certain why, and he didn't like it worth a shit. Human females were always trouble. There was no actual mating involved. They weren't of the 'people'. One fucked them and left them and he'd done so plenty of times without a backward glance. He had the uncomfortable suspicion, though, that his desire for this human female was different.

Actually, he knew it was different and that was what was plaguing him.

He hadn't *just* felt the heat of desire every time he'd looked at her and felt her touch, watched her dance. He'd felt possessiveness. He'd felt protective in a way he hadn't with any female of the tribe of man-children before, or even of his own tribe. He'd felt protective to the point of stupidity.

He'd given himself away to his captors because that bastard Panas had hit her. If he could've gotten hold of him then he would have torn him limb from limb and it had had nothing to do with what the man had done to him. Nothing. He hadn't given a thought to anything beyond protecting *her*.

He ground his teeth in irritation. As little as he liked accepting the feelings churning in his belly, as hard as he was working to deny any of it, he knew the things he felt couldn't be dismissed as just desire. He could feel the mating fever working through his mind and gaining ground.

He could not mate *her*, he thought angrily. She was human. It wasn't possible.

Actually, his mind argued, it *was* according to what he'd heard—just unlikely. There was no 'turning' a human. If they were born human, they *remained* human, no matter how assiduously a beast-man fucked them and, without that possibility, there was also no possibility of a true mating. The female was never going to nurture his seed and therefore never going to bond with him. A beast-man might bond with her if he was insane enough to hang around, or unfortunate enough to find himself enthralled by a human female—but the most likely scenario was that he would find himself bonded to a female who didn't return his sentiments.

He had heard that it was possible to mate with a human female if the female formed an attachment to the beast-man, but he didn't know of any instances first hand where that had happened and he strongly suspected it was just a myth.

The other scenario not only wasn't a myth, however, he'd known of males that got burned—got so attached to the human female they hadn't been able to turn away from her, or leave, and they'd ended up dead.

Because sooner or later, if a beast-man walked among the man-children, the man-children discovered what he was—or they caught him in his beast form and killed or captured him and caged him because he was a 'dangerous' beast and they didn't allow dangerous beasts too close to them.

The female was trouble—more than most—especially to him. If he was smart, he'd leave it at the kiss and steer clear.

He had a bad feeling, though, that the impulse that had driven him to kiss her was just the tip of the iceberg. One taste was not going to be enough for him. He could already feel the hunger building. Inside, his instincts warred with his logic. One side was goading him to follow his desires, to assuage his need of her. The other was warning him against it, warning him there'd be no alleviating it, that he would only be building a greater hunger with each taste.

* * * *

Sergei's fury didn't abate a good deal despite his efforts to wrestle it to a more manageable level by assuring himself the fucking lion-man would only get his just deserts if he couldn't keep his hands off of the female. He'd been young still when his parents had died, but he had not been so far from maturity that his father had failed to educate him about mating.

In point of fact, much to his everlasting sorrow and guilt, it was the onset of his maturity that had led to his parents' death.

He'd not only lost the ability to control his shifts from man to beast and back again, he'd become so fascinated with the human females—which were the *only* females anywhere around—he'd become infatuated with one to the point that he'd begun to stalk her with an eye to claiming her as his mate.

He'd kept it from his parents, knowing they would disapprove, knowing they would remove him from temptation if they had any idea how fascinated he was with the beautiful little blond girl that had taken his fancy.

He hadn't realized, then, that human females did not reach the maturity to mate at quite the same age—did not in fact *choose* mates as his tribe did. She had not been unwilling for all that. She had encouraged him.

Unfortunately, her parents had objected.

Equally unfortunate, he'd been so worked up by the time they'd been discovered his passions had instantly been diverted to rage and possessiveness when the girl's father had attacked him. He'd shifted, without thought, into his true form. He hadn't killed. He'd been too intent on escaping the scene of his humiliation, too intent on escaping his father's wrath to realize, in time, that he hadn't just given himself away. He'd given his parents away.

Despite all the warnings his parents had peeled over his head his entire life, he hadn't really believed humans would react so violently to the discovery. They'd killed both of his parents, attacking them without warning, before he'd realized he had to confess what he'd done and gone home.

He'd barely escaped with his own life.

He'd wondered for a long while why he'd bothered. He deserved to die. He'd been the cause of his parents' deaths.

His internal will to live had been stronger than his guilt, though. His body had healed so that his mind could torment him forever more with what he'd done.

And, in time, the same instincts that had brought about disaster, had resurrected themselves to torment him along with the guilt. It had been a stronger drive, though, one he couldn't control or ignore.

It had led him here.

This time it was going to get him killed if he didn't control it.

Kate was human. If he could just keep that in the forefront of his mind and ignore the burning need roiling in his gut, he might live long enough to overcome it.

He would be much better off, he knew, if he could just ignore the possessiveness that clouded his mind every time the lion-man looked at Kate.

Let him have her and all the trouble that went with her, he thought, trying to ignore the sick rage that welled anew each time he thought about it.

Chapter Five

By the time the sun was fully up, Kate was beginning to feel desperate. She knew better than to whine, though, when Sergei had already nearly bitten her head off for talking too much. By her best guesstimate, they'd been walking for more than two hours—if you could call what they were doing walking. *She* didn't call it walking. Although the pace they set fell short of jogging—for them—she was forced to walk as fast as she could and then jog in spurts when they outdistanced her.

And every time she broke into a jog, one or the other, or both, would turn and glare at her for making too much noise.

A swift death almost began to look more appealing than the torture she was enduring.

And the grim reality was that she was probably going to go through hell and *still* catch a bullet.

She didn't realize they were climbing at first. The ground was uneven anyway, and she was more focused on keeping up—when her mind wasn't on her aches and pains, the hunger gnawing at her belly, her parched throat, and the ever expanding girth of her bladder.

She supposed it was ridiculous to be so shy about relieving herself when she did a nightly gig exposing everything she had, but, absurd or not, she was uncomfortable with the idea. Add to that the fact that she had a real problem with squatting in the woods and she couldn't even think about trying without also imagining one or both of the cats pouncing on her just about the time she got her britches down and death by bladder explosion seemed preferable to giving it a try.

No way were the Neanderthals she was following going to actually wait on her.

They stumbled upon a trickling brook just about the time she'd decided she was going to expire from dehydration. Despite the fact that it was running over dirt, she felt her heart leap and then take a nose dive to her toes. The sound of the running water by itself was enough to increase her discomfort by leaps and bounds and she knew if she drank any she'd be in worse shape.

As Sergei and Silvair crouched by the edge of the brook, scooping up handfuls of water to drink, she watched them yearningly, trying to gather enough spit in her mouth to dampen her throat. After a moment, Sergei straightened, walked a few paces down stream and whipped it out to relieve himself. Silvair followed him a few moments later.

This, Kate decided, staring at their backs, was the *only* time a woman felt penis envy, contrary to what that idiot Sigmund thought. It was also the one occasion in a man's life where he could enjoy lording it over a woman that he had a built in hose for his comfort.

Neither of them did, but they didn't have to. She felt the resentment just the same.

Both men glanced at her when they returned to drink more water.

Kate stared stonily into the distance, refusing to watch them drink this time.

"You should relieve yourself and drink. Ve vill be moving again soon. Dere is no more vater nearby."

She didn't know how Silvair could possibly know that, but he said it with such conviction that the dryness in her throat and mouth magnified to an agonizing degree.

She couldn't stand it!

Putting a little distance between herself and them, she looked around for a likely looking hiding spot and finally stripped off her jeans, tennis shoes, and panties. She didn't glance back at them. She knew they would be glaring at her for stripping down just to pee, but she wasn't taking any chances with the only clothes she had. Placing them on a rock, she surveyed the area carefully for any sign of the missing felines and then stepped cautiously behind the trunk of a pine.

Both men were staring in her direction when she came from behind the tree, standing so stiffly alert that she felt the hairs on the back of her neck lift. Whipping her head around, she scanned the woods for the cats again. She didn't see them, but she was still unnerved. Grabbing up her clothing, she hurried back to Silvair and Sergei, throwing uneasy glances over her shoulder as she went.

"Did you see something?" she asked a little breathlessly when she reached them.

When neither man answered, she turned to look up at them.

They weren't staring into the distance anymore.

They were staring down at her naked pussy, their faces taut.

Feeling foolish, irritated, and mildly embarrassed by their focus, Kate shifted her bundle lower to cover herself. The moment the 'curtain' came down, both men lifted their gaze from her mound to her face. A wave of heat rolled over her at the raw need in both men's eyes. She'd had men look at her with desire. She'd even felt a flicker of interest a few times when men had looked at her like that. She hadn't felt weak all over, though, hadn't felt their hunger as almost a tangible thing.

Both men surged toward her at once, stopped, and turned to glare at each other.

Kate's stomach executed a somersault as the men gripped each others arms, their faces instantly transformed from lust to rage.

"I'll do you both!" Kate gasped out quickly before she even realized the thought was there. She regretted it almost the moment the words were out, but she knew they were within a hair's breadth of a royal battle and she didn't want to become the 'spoils of war'.

Their heads whipped in her direction the moment she spoke, their gazes zeroing in and narrowing on the object of their desires—not her, her pussy.

She swallowed hard when their heads swiveled toward one another once more, realizing the offering wasn't going to prevent a fight. *Now* they were going to fight over who was first.

Dropping her clothes, she whirled to flee the scene. "The first one to catch ... ugh!"

The body that slammed into her felt like a truck. Her head swam as she was snatched off her feet and twirled in a circle.

By the time her head stopped spinning she found herself falling toward the ground. Fully expecting to feel the grind of rocks and dirt on her bare back and buttocks when she landed, she was surprised to feel the cool, relative softness of grasses, or maybe moss, instead.

The surprise and recognition was brief, however. Silvair covered her mouth in ravaging assault before she could do more than gasp for breath.

She knew that mouth, had learned the intoxicating essence of Silvair in their one brief encounter earlier and her body responded instantly to his summoning of her heat, lighting up for him, electrifying her senses. Blood surged into her nether regions as she felt him groping between them to free his engorged member from his jeans. Moisture followed the flow, coating her channel and dampening her nether lips even as she felt the hard caress of the head of his cock along her cleft.

He grunted with satisfaction as he engaged his body with hers and curled his hips to breach the reluctant yielding of her flesh to his. She sucked in a harsh breath, filling her lungs with his breath as she felt him stretching her. It sent another dizzying, pleasurable wave through her.

He gave her no time to think, to allow room for doubts or uncertainty. Wrenching his mouth from hers, he drove into her with even, steady, determined pressure until he'd sheathed his flesh so deeply inside of her she was gasping for breath. Quakes trembled along the walls of her sex as he embedded himself to the hilt inside of her and followed his retreat as he withdrew his flesh to drive into her again.

Her flesh stippled at the exquisiteness of the pleasure rippling along the walls of her channel with his rhythmic thrust and retreat. She released a low groan as she felt her body tighten with anticipation. A shudder went through his big body at the sound. He let out a harsh breath and began to move faster, stoking the fire inside her, stroking the walls of her channel until, abruptly, the building anticipation expanded beyond her control and her body began to convulsive in hard spasms of release. He covered her mouth, absorbing her keen cries of ecstasy as she came.

Shuddering as her body kneaded his flesh, he uttered a hoarse groan into her mouth and followed her, his whole body jerking as it expelled his seed into her.

She was still gasping for breath, drifting in the semi-consciousness of heated aftermath, when he withdrew and rolled away.

He'd scarcely done so when Sergei took his place, falling upon her with all the ravening hunger Silvair had. Shoving her shirt and bra upward, he tugged greedily at her puckered, sensitive nipples, dragging a reluctant groan from her as she felt her body surge upward, igniting as if the fire hadn't just been quenched. She clutched as his head, of half a mind to shove him away at the nearly unbearable sensations rocking her.

She was too sensitive, she thought a little wildly. She hadn't had the chance to catch her breath or come down from the euphoric high Silvair had taken her to.

He was insistent, however, hungry, feeding his own needs, and her body responded with a will of its own, regardless of her certainty that she couldn't bear to feel more. She was nearly sobbing for breath when he ceased to suckle her breasts and covered her mouth with his.

Heat poured through her veins in a scouring tide when he did, when he filled her mouth and her senses with himself, his taste, the gratifying stroke of his tongue along hers. He broke the kiss after only a moment, shifting upward to impale her on his cock.

She groaned when she felt him stretching her almost to the point of pain, wondering a little wildly if her body would split as his girth continued to press against the walls of her channel until he'd conquered the sensitive pathway and he began to stroke her with almost punishing thrusts. Opening her eyes, she peered up at the hard wall of chest above her, watching the play of muscles in his chest and arms as he drove into her again and again.

The force and suddenness of her climax dragged a sharp cry from her. She bit her lip, trying to contain the sound as the second wave hit her, groaning instead. He settled more heavily against her as his own body seized in climax, shaking with the force of it, uttering a choked, guttural groan.

The moment Kate's body ceased to spasm it seemed every ounce of strength left her. Limp with repletion, she struggled for a moment to fend off the descent of darkness around her and then simply gave in to it.

She roused when Sergei withdrew from her, but with only a vague awareness of anything beyond herself. Her entire being seemed focused inwardly, on the struggle to catch her breath, to regulate her pounding heart, to revel in the glorious aftermath of being well and truly fucked within an inch of her life. Inwardly, she smiled. Outwardly, she couldn't even summon enough strength to curl her lips.

A shiver skated through her when he left her but she would've been perfectly content to lay right where she was and sleep. Darkness descended, however, so abruptly that she struggled and finally managed to lift her eyelids enough to peer through her lashes.

Silvair and Sergei were leaning over her, staring down at her with almost identical expressions of consternation. "You are hurt?" Sergei asked in a gruff voice.

She frowned in concentration, summoning enough mental power for an inventory. "No," she finally said weakly.

"Ve can not say he-uh," Silvair said after a moment.

Kate groaned, brought very reluctantly back to reality. All she wanted to do was sleep. She'd been tired before. She was past tired now. Sucking in a deep breath, she struggled to gather the strength to rise and finally managed to push herself up to a sitting position. Dizzy with fatigue, she looked at the brook a short distance away longingly. Her parched throat closed.

She wasn't going anywhere until she'd had water. She didn't care if it was dirty. It was wet. Her knees wobbled and threatened to buckle when she pushed herself to her feet, but she made it to the water. Kneeling on the rough ground, she winced at the pain that shot through her knees but leaned down to scoop water up to drink anyway. It was icy cold, she discovered with surprise, and it felt wonderful sliding down her throat.

When she'd drank her fill, she splashed the water over her face and then over her genitals. She didn't know which was the most eye opening experience, ice water on her heated face, or icy water on her still throbbing nether lips. She was wide awake, however, by the time she'd dabbled in the icy water for a few moments.

She was still weak for all that and it took all she could do to get to her feet and look around for her clothes.

Sergei and Silvair, she discovered, were watching her with a mixture of doubt, irritation—and lust. She sent them both a narrow eyed glare—which they missed because their gazes were trained on her pussy.

If she could speak through *those* lips, she thought irritably, she might catch their attention.

It was probably because it was bare, she decided. 'Bush' was a no-no for exotic dancers, however, even a neatly trimmed one—at least at Panas' club. She'd had it waxed so many times, she'd forgotten what color her pubic hair was. Straightening her bra and shirt as she moved away from the brook, she bent over and retrieved her panties, shaking the dirt from them before she slipped them on. Her legs were still so wobbly from Sergei and Silvair playing 'make a wish' it took all she could do to get her jeans on.

She was looking around for a place to sit down to put her shoes on when Sergei strode toward her and scooped her into his arms, lifting her against his chest. She looked at his face with surprise and more than a little uneasiness. He didn't return her questioning look. Instead, after glancing around, he moved to the streambed and waded in, turning upstream.

Expecting any minute that he would trip over something and sprawl out, dunking her in the water, Kate dropped her shoes onto her belly and looped her arms around his neck to hold on. Silvair waded in behind them, but after a few minutes, he moved up to walk alongside them and then pulled ahead, leading the way.

When Sergei continued to walk as surefooted as if he was on flat ground and showed no inclination to put her down to walk on her own, Kate finally settled her head on his shoulder.

After a few minutes, she found herself drifting toward sleep again. She didn't try to fight it.

* * * *

There had not been a lot of time when he was clear headed enough to do so, but Sergei was sure he'd evaluated the situation carefully since they had left the club and come up with the best possible plan. He'd allowed his burning need to avenge himself to overrule his judgment when he'd found his cage open and the opportunity he'd been waiting for, true, and he had the uneasy feeling that that had been a serious error in judgment even though the things Kate had told him seemed to indicate otherwise. He hadn't considered, at the time, that he was making certain that he remained free, but in exacting his revenge he had also insured that he didn't have to worry about Panas or any of his men coming after him.

The authorities were another matter. They were bound to investigate and also bound to arrive at the conclusion that no man was responsible for the deaths at the club.

They would be searching for him and Silvair, now, both as men and as beasts and because they had killed, however justified the taking of lives had been, they would be searching to kill, not merely to capture them again.

That had been the mistake—changing—but he still didn't see any way they could've avoided it. They were both too far from their homeland to make it back in their beast forms. They would need money, and they would have to walk among the men-children to make their way. They could not do that in beast form, could not have even if they had not stood out as not belonging here at all.

Taking Kate had been his next mistake.

He still wasn't completely certain of why he had.

He had certainly not thought it through. He could tell himself that he'd forgotten in all the years since he'd lived among humans just how weak they were, and that was true. He *had* forgotten, but that wasn't the reason he'd taken her anymore than the need he'd felt to protect her was true. He'd killed Panas. He'd eliminated the reason she needed protecting.

And beyond that, she wasn't his to protect, not his responsibility and not *his* woman.

She was a danger to him in more ways than he could count.

She'd struggled to keep up with him and Silvair. She hadn't complained. She hadn't gone out of her way to mark their trail.

But she was human. She couldn't help it anymore than she could help slowing them down.

And the very fact that he had taken her would make the authorities more determined to find them.

He could have rectified that situation by leaving her once they'd evaded the two men who'd been shooting at them. Both had been injured. He was fairly sure they wouldn't have been able to follow for long and that she would've been safe from them.

He hadn't been completely certain, though, and he hadn't been able to bring himself to risk it.

He had a bad feeling, though, that none of the reasons he'd made up in his mind that had sounded so logical were his true motive for bringing her along. All of them were true and any one of them was a good enough reason to have done what he'd done. They just weren't the actual motivation—or rather they were an extension of the true reason.

He was obsessed with the woman. He was as certain as he could be that it was purely on a sexual level and it wasn't hard to figure that one out. She was beautiful and desirable, even if she was human.

Beyond that, she was his first woman.

If he had been with others, even a few others, he thought he might not have been quite so enthralled. He had been trying to convince himself ever since that first coupling that there was nothing exceptional about it *except* for the fact that he hadn't experienced it before. If he coupled with another woman, human or of his tribe, it would feel just as good—perhaps even better, although he had a very hard time imagining 'better' when being inside of her made him feel as if he'd died and gone to heaven.

He grew hard again just thinking about it, just as he had every time he had thought about it since that first time. It would have been a blessing if he had discovered when he took her again that he'd only imagined how good it had felt, that the drugs had somehow made it seem far better than it actually was. Instead, he had discovered that, without the drugs dulling his senses—in his man form—it had surpassed that first experience.

All he had wanted to do when he had expended himself was to begin again—right then.

He had been in a fever of impatience for Silvair to be done so that he could have her and he still wasn't sure why he had even *allowed* Silvair to have her first.

Actually, he was. He had known that if he took the time to beat Silvair down he would not *also* have the time to fuck her and beyond that time consideration, he had feared, in the back of his mind, that she would refuse to have him if he killed Silvair first and also that there was a possibility that she could be hurt since she was too close to the battle ground.

Waiting had seemed like the only thing he *could* do when he couldn't really focus on anything beyond having her as quickly as possible.

Which was yet another reason she was a danger to him. She addled his wits.

It worried him that she was so much weaker after he and Silvair had coupled with her. His memory was definitely faulty—it had been *years* after all since he'd had such close contact with humans—and he hadn't been much more than a cub at the time, but he didn't recall them being *this* weak.

Maybe that was the perception of his youth? *He* was stronger now, bigger and far stronger than he'd been when he'd left the human world. Maybe he and Silvair hadn't actually done her any harm?

He could tell Silvair had been disturbed by it, though, and he'd gotten the impression that Silvair was not only more experienced than him with females—not at all difficult when he had not even been with one before Kate—but also with humans in general. He wasn't certain that was true. They hadn't exactly taken the time to get to know one another when they had waded through Panas and his men.

And he was older than Silvair.

It rankled that he was older than Silvair and far less experienced.

He wondered if Silvair could tell.

More importantly, could Kate tell?

Would she choose Silvair over him because he had a better understanding of how to please?

An understanding, he corrected himself. He had only his instincts to guide him, no knowledge or experience.

The one time he had *almost* coupled hardly counted. The girl had had no more notion of what they were doing than he had.

He shook those thoughts off after a little while. He had no business allowing such things to clutter his mind, which was yet another reason the woman was a danger to him. He should be focused on survival, not worrying about whether she'd found his touch as pleasurable as he had found hers.

He moved up beside Silvair once they had followed the brook far enough he was certain it would throw the dogs off their scent. "We will have to leave Kate if we are to confuse the trackers," he said in a low voice he hoped would not awaken her.

Chapter Six

Silvair glanced at Kate's sleeping face and then at Sergei. It made sense, more sense than trying to drag her along with them, but he felt a strong surge of reluctance even as he acknowledged that Sergei was right. "I am tinking same ting, but I doan like it," he responded finally. "Ve are long vay from man-children. I've not caught any scent at all. She's a pretty little ting, but veak and helpless, I'm tinking. More dan most."

Sergei felt his gut clench at Silvair's comments. "Da, but I had thought only for a little while. I won't leave her here. She would not find her way back and she would die. I'm tinking we should find a place where she'll be safe while we lose de dogs. Den, we come back, we decide what to do wid her."

Silvair considered that. "Goot idea, but dere is a cat here. I have caught de scent several times. I vill stay wid her while you confuse de trail, and den you can stay while I do de same."

Sergei discovered he didn't particularly like the idea of leaving her with Silvair, even it if was only for a little while. From a purely practical standpoint, it made sense. He'd caught the scent of the cat, too. It hadn't particularly bothered him because he knew it wouldn't be a problem for him, even though he'd begun to suspect the cat was stalking them.

He found that confusing. There was nothing about the scent to suggest that it was man-beast as he and Silvair were and if it was no more than beast it should have turned away once it caught their scent, not followed them.

The only explanation that came to mind was that it was a man-eater and, if he was right, that was only one more reason not to let Kate out of their sight.

And he still didn't like the idea of leaving her with Silvair.

"Dere is no udder way," Silvair said, voicing his own thoughts.

Sergei nodded, tamping his reluctance, which he knew had more to do with the fact that he suspected the lion-man was as hungry for Kate as he was. He didn't know the man, but he'd sensed nothing about him that suggested he was untrustworthy. He didn't believe Silvair would abandon her or fail to protect her if the need arose.

He also, unfortunately, didn't doubt that Silvair would use the opportunity to better acquaint himself with Kate unless she objected, and she wasn't showing any particular preference for either one of them.

Even if she did have a preference, he didn't think she would object. Panas had not been the sort of man who took objections well. If Kate had been with him very long he had probably taught her it was unwise to object.

That was one of the things, he realized, that had been bothering him since he had taken her. She had not chosen him—or Silvair for that matter. She had offered herself, he strongly suspected, because she had been afraid they would take regardless of her wishes and she had been afraid of the consequences, to her, if they had fought over her.

That knowledge, or at least suspicion, had given rise to a dissatisfaction that had nothing to do with the act itself. He had enjoyed that thoroughly. She had behaved as if she was willing. She had, in fact, behaved as if she had enjoyed it.

He wasn't as certain as he would've liked to be that it was real and not just an act to avoid unpleasantness, though.

He also wasn't altogether certain of why it was that the possibility was so repugnant to him. *He* had enjoyed it regardless, and he would not be here very long if he could help it. He meant to be as far from this place as he could get as quickly as he could go—which meant leaving Kate behind. In the scheme of things, what did it matter how willing or unwilling she was so long as she gave him what he wanted while he was with her?

It did matter, though. It displeased him. It left him feeling as if he was somehow missing something important.

It was some consolation that what could be said for him could also be said for Silvair—but not much.

He would work harder to please her, he decided, and then he would not feel as if he had somehow failed and the sense of dissatisfaction wouldn't plague him.

* * * *

Kate wasn't certain what had aroused her, but she didn't think it was the fact that she'd had enough sleep. It was still daylight when she woke, and hours from dusk. Maybe, she thought, it was just that it was around the time she usually woke?

"You are awake?"

Reluctantly, Kate acknowledged the question by lifting her head. It wasn't just because she was still tired, though, and more inclined to go back to sleep than rouse completely. It felt good being held by him, comforting, and she was reluctant to give up that sense of security, however misguided it was. He smelled good, too, not perfumy—not that she had a thing against that. Some of the men's colognes got her hot sniffing them right from the bottle. But his scent was 'undressed up', all his, and it was nice—just a light, clean, healthy smell. "Yes," she said, discovering her voice was still husky with sleep.

"You can walk now?"

She nodded, immediately embarrassed by the fact that she'd let him carry her—god only knew how far or how long. She staggered slightly when he set her on her feet, wincing as the tender soles of her bare feet touched the rocky soil. Grasping his arm to steady herself, she slipped her tennis shoes on.

That was when she noticed that he—both men—were barefooted.

She hadn't actually questioned why it was that neither one of them were wearing more than jeans—no shirt, no shoes, no underwear. It didn't seem to bother either one of them, so undoubtedly they were used to going around barefooted, but still ….

They hadn't gone *in* to the club dressed like that.

She slid a speculative glance up at Sergei. There was only one explanation that came readily to mind—they'd been with some of the 'girls'. That didn't explain how they'd gone from getting 'serviced' to robbing the place, though. Even if they'd used that as an excuse to get in to start with, why hadn't they dressed *before* they'd robbed Panas?

"You never did tell me what you and Silvair were doing in the club?" she asked hesitantly.

Sergei's face closed instantly.

"Not that it's any of my business," Kate added hurriedly.

"Silvair will take you dere."

Kate followed the direction of his pointing finger, but she didn't see anything. Nothing, that is but more of the same— pines, rocky soil, scrubby bushes here and there.

She glanced at Silvair and then Sergei, feeling her belly tighten with uneasiness. "What's up there?" she asked a little hoarsely.

Sergei's lips tightened. "A place to wait."

She glanced in the direction he'd indicated again, but she still didn't see anything. She did feel something, though, fear. Neither of the men were carrying guns. She knew that, but she flicked a nervous glance over them anyway, looking for a telltale bulge in their pockets that might be a small pistol or a knife. She licked suddenly dry lips. "If it's just too much trouble to have me along, I could go down that way," she said, pointing in the opposite direction. "I'm sure I could find my way ... somewhere. And I wouldn't tell anybody anything. Actually, I couldn't, because I'm not a woods person and I was asleep anyway, and I haven't any idea where we are."

"We doan mean to harm you, Sveety," Silvair said gruffly. "I vill stay and take care of you and den, vhen Sergei come back, I vill go and lay out anudder trail to confuse de trackers."

"Take care?" Kate asked nervously, feeling somewhat reassured, though she didn't particularly like the way he'd said 'take care of'.

"Ja," he said, nodding. "Protect."

They hadn't offered to hurt her and yet it popped into her mind instantly to wonder if they'd just wanted to get her deep enough into the woods nobody would hear her scream.

If she'd thought of that before .... She would've just spent the last several hours terrified out of her mind instead of just scared. She hadn't been out of their sight since they'd taken her or far enough away to have had a chance of outrunning either one of them, let alone both.

She nodded jerkily because there didn't seem to be an option, starting toward Silvair, hoping he would turn as he had before and walk off, expecting her to follow. Instead, he waited for her to reach him before he turned and began to climb the slope upward. Kate glanced back as she reached him. Sergei was standing where she'd left him, watching her.

She wished she could've interpreted his expression, but it was hard to read anything from it.

She didn't glance at Silvair again. She tried to focus on looking calm, relaxed, unsuspecting. She tried to dawdle without appearing to do so. After a few moments, she glanced back toward Sergei again and discovered he'd disappeared—completely. She paused, scanning the area, but he'd vanished like a puff of smoke.

She didn't have to worry about him, she told herself.

She just wished she'd seen which direction he'd taken.

She couldn't think about that right now, she decided. She had to focus on escaping whatever it was they had in mind. Toward that end, she flicked a few glances around, trying to decide the best direction to run. Not the way they'd just come. Sergei was that way—somewhere. Not the direction she'd pointed out.

Or maybe it would be a better idea to head that way after all? Surely they'd think she wouldn't go the way she'd already pointed out?

She had a bad feeling Silvair knew she meant to run. He kept pace with her.

After a few minutes, she noticed something she hadn't before. A jumble of rocks close to the summit of the hill they were climbing formed a cave of sorts—or at least appeared to. There was a dark opening that hinted at depth.

Her heart leapt into her throat and tried to strangle her. She felt alternately hot and then cold.

Waiting until they were within a few yards of the jumble of rocks, Kate sucked in a deep breath, whirled, and ran for all she was worth down the hill they'd just climbed. The incline gave her more speed than she might otherwise have managed.

And it still didn't do her one bit of good!

Her charge was cut short by an arm snaking around her waist before she'd even managed to achieve full speed. She didn't know how he was able to keep their combined momentum from sending them both plowing into the gravelly dirt, or rolling down the hill, but somehow he did. Instead, he used her own momentum to swing her around and into the cage of his body and arms. She struggled with grim, mindless determination to break free of his grip as he hauled her back up the hill, too focused on clawing at his hands and arms even to think to scream.

She remembered her voice as he dragged her into the cave formed by the boulders, but, almost as if he'd anticipated it, knew what she intended the moment she sucked in a sharp breath, he covered her mouth with his hand, covered most of her face. She hadn't realized just how big his hands were until he planted the palm over her lower face and it covered her mouth, nose, and most of her eyes. More panic shot through her when she tried to suck in another breath and discovered she couldn't breathe. She kicked and flailed her arms wildly.

Somewhere in her battle to free herself and his to hold on her, they tumbled into the dirt just inside the cave. Kate sucked in several harsh breaths when he removed his hand from her mouth to grab her wrists instead, bearing them down to the dirt.

"Kate!" he growled. "Be still! I vill not hurt you!"

She stilled, not because she believed him but because she ran out of any strength to fight him. Struggling for breath as the weight of his chest compressed hers, she stared up at him in wild eyed fear in the shadowy interior of the cave.

"I von't hurt you!"

"Promise?" she gasped finally on a quavering voice, feeling tears clog her throat.

He released his grip on her wrists. Shifting his weight to one side of her, he framed her face in the crook between his thumb and forefinger. "I did not bring you here to hurt you. Ve must stay out of sight."

She sniffed back the sting of tears, feeling the beginnings of relief. "You mean it? That's all ... that's why ...?"

He shook his head at her. "You are certain you are not feline?" he asked smiling faintly now.

Kate swallowed with an effort, flicking a glance down at his chest and arms, seeing for the first time the results of her battle. She'd scratched him all over, drawn blood in several places. She could hardly believe he could take it so calmly let alone joke about it. Remorse filled her. He must think she'd lost her mind! "I'm sorry!" she said on a voice that quavered on the edge of a wail.

"Shhh! *I* am sorry," he murmured, stroking her cheek. "I frightened you, ja? I could not let you give us away."

He studied her for a long moment and finally dropped his head forward, rubbing his cheek along hers. A sound, almost like a purr rumbled from his chest as he stroked her cheek with his. The heat of his breath against her ear as he nuzzled the sensitive shell created a rippling tide of goosebumps along her neck and down to her breasts, making her nipples pucker and stand erect, making her belly tighten with a surge of anticipation.

When he lifted his head slightly and fitted his lips to hers, it seemed the most natural thing in the world to open her mouth to his caress. Relief surged through her at the heat of his mouth, the intimate invasion of his tongue. Hard upon the heels of that a languid heat invaded her. She surged upward to meet him as she sensed his withdrawal in the lightening of pressure on her mouth, as hungry for reassurance as the passion his kiss promised, lifting her arms to pull him closer as she entwined her tongue with his in an intimate duel that established maximum contact. His taste filled her like a magical elixir, a heady brew that chased the chill of her fear from her bones and replaced it with fire, scattering her chaotic thoughts in a dizzying whirlwind.

Her pursuit or the sound of complaint she made in her throat when he would've withdrawn sent a shudder rippling through the hard body pressed to her. He almost seemed to hesitate for a fraction of a second and then the entire tone of his kiss transformed in an instant from soothing apology to ravenous demand. Lifting away fractionally, he realigned the fit of their mouths and settled his more firmly against hers, coaxing her tongue into his mouth to suckle it greedily for many moments before he released captivity of it and delved into the heated cavern of her mouth again, exploring every surface with a thoroughness that left her shaking and breathless.

His golden eyes glowed with an inner fire when he lifted his head and met her gaze for a heart-stopping moment before his gaze moved down to her breasts. Lifting away from her abruptly, he grasped the hem of her shirt with shaking hands and peeled it off over her head. Skimming his hands lightly over her shoulders, breasts, and ribcage, he frowned as he studied the bra and then unhooked the front closure, capturing her breasts as they fell free of restraint and kneading them in his hands.

She'd thought her breasts full enough, but the size of his hands dwarfed them as he squeezed both at once, studying the puckered, erect tips with keen interest but making no attempt to touch them as she ached for him to. Releasing her breasts after only a moment, he skimmed his hands down her ribs again with obvious impatience and worked the closure of her jeans free, hooking his thumbs into the waistband and tugging them off her hips along with her panties as he came up on his knees.

When he'd stripped her bare, he simply sat back on his heels for a prolonged moment, allowing his gaze to wander over the flesh he'd bared. A fine tremor ran through the hands he settled on her thighs and skated upward to the juncture, stroking her nether lips lightly with his thumbs before he parted them to study the darker pink inner lips.

Kate sucked in a shuddering breath and held it, watching his face as he studied her, feeling her entire body tighten as his face grew taut, his eyes darkening. He swallowed thickly. "My pretty little Kate has a pretty little ting here," he murmured, dragging his gaze from his inspection after a moment to meet her gaze as he leaned over her.

He rubbed his chest along her body sinuously, burrowing his face along one shoulder and the side of her neck and breathing deeply, merely rubbing body to body, twisting his face restlessly against her sensitive skin as if he was trying to gather the scent of her skin onto his. A rumbling groan issued from deep in his chest. Abruptly, he scooped his arms beneath her shoulders and sat back on his heels again, pulling her with him.

Weak already with the desire coursing through her, her head lolled limply on her shoulders as he did so. He took advantage of her exposed throat, lathing it with his tongue from the base to the edge of her jaw before he sought her mouth and captured it beneath his again. The roughness of his jeans against the sensitive skin of her nether lips as he dragged her onto his thighs sent a shiver through her. Supporting her shoulders with one arm, he slipped the other down her back to cup and knead her buttocks and then dragged her against his erection and held her tightly as he undulated his hips, pressing his hard length against her cleft and easing rhythmically as he thrust his tongue into her mouth and retreated in sync.

Shivering, she looped her arms around his shoulders to steady herself, arching her back to draw herself closer to him. The tips of her breasts brushed his hard chest with each movement. The friction of skin to skin sent electrifying impulses from the bundled nerve endings in her nipples to her womb, making it tighten and relax in an echoing rhythm that superheated the gathering fire inside her until she felt as if she would go up in flames, pass out from the darkness encroaching on her mind.

Intoxicated with need, impatience moved through her, the need to feel his cock embedded deeply inside of her. Her throat closed with hunger. Her sex quaked with want, wept with neglect. As if he read her mind, he slipped his hand from her hips after a moment and released his cock from the prison of his jeans. He was panting harshly as he broke the kiss, urging her up on her knees to align their bodies.

Shaking all over, she struggled to comply, sucking in a harsh breath as she felt the hard knob of the head of his cock connect with her opening, delve inside of her. He caught her hips with his hands, tipping his head down to watch as he speared her flesh with his own, thrusting and retreating shallowly until he'd coated his shaft with her juices and then thrusting hard to breach her depths.

She squeezed her eyes shut, her breath catching in her throat as she sank at last to the hilt of his cock and felt a fluttering response deep inside of her. His arms tightened around her, plastering her against his body, holding her still while her body adjusted to his girth or perhaps only to savor the sensation himself. His breath came in short, harsh, almost pained gasps as he held her. The faint tremors she'd felt rippling through him became harder until he was shaking all over. "Goot, Kate. You feel so goot," he groaned. "I vant to stay just like dis forever."

The words were no sooner said, though, when he uttered a harsh groan. Lifting a hand to spear his fingers through her hair, he dragged her head back and ravished her mouth in a brief, searing kiss and then tore his mouth from hers and began to move with a feverish sort of desperation in short, deep, jerking jabs that communicated itself to her body and sent it spiraling out of control. She uttered a sob as a warning spasm rippled along the muscles of her channel, making them fist tighter around his thick flesh. He groaned and shuddered in counter, lifting and pounding into her harder and faster in a way that swiftly sent her body into hard paroxysms of ecstasy that dragged choked cries from her.

He uttered a growling groan, shook, and spilled his hot seed into her passage.

Kate's release expended everything—the fear of before, the tension, the last ounce of energy. Dropping her head weakly to his shoulder, she let go, sinking into semi-consciousness, barely aware of the soothing, appreciative stroke of his hands over her, even less aware as he finally eased her away from him and settled her on her clothes on the ground. Her last spark of awareness was the touch of his hand as he smoothed her hair from her cheeks and then she sank into complete nothingness, seeking the rest she'd been denied by their flight into the wilderness.

Chapter Seven

A low, threatening rumble awoke Kate. She opened her eyes with an effort and discovered the shadows within the 'lair' had deepened. Disoriented from sleep, it took her a few moments to figure out where she was and then, after she'd identified the rough rock walls, to remember how and why she'd gotten where she was.

She sat up abruptly in alarm as she heard movement at the mouth of the tiny cave. Sergei squeezed into the opening, completely filling it for a moment and making the cave even darker. When he'd pushed through, she saw that he was scowling fiercely and breathing heavily, as if from exertion.

Guilt instantly filled her at the savage light in his golden eyes, not fear, though she didn't identify the source of the guilt immediately.

The cave wreaked of sex, though.

And she was naked.

The scan of Sergei's gaze brought that into her mind before her own senses registered it.

There were reddened fist sized patches on his chest and another on one high cheekbone. The discolorations connected with the previously unidentified meaty impacts she'd heard and growls of effort. Before her sluggish brain could completely settle on the obvious indications of a scuffle, he drew her attention to the picnic basket he held in his hand as he plunked it to the ground angrily and settled on his buttocks, examining one arm.

His attention drew hers and she noticed with a start that there was a blackened hole in his upper arm oozing blood sluggishly. Making a sound of consternation when she realized what it was, she surged toward him. "You were shot!" she gasped, catching his arm and examining the wound more closely. "Sergei! What happened?"

His face was taut when she met his gaze—tight with a mixture of both pain and anger. Some of it eased, though, as he studied her anxious face.

"Did you ... did you see some of Panas' men?"

Briefly, he looked downright sheepish. "*Nyet*," he growled irritably.

She glanced from his arm to the picnic basket and drew her own conclusions.

His color was faintly heightened when she met his gaze again. Finally, he shrugged. "It was there and ... I was hungry."

It was the truth, or at least part of it. He *was* hungry, but he hadn't been thinking of his own empty stomach at the time. There was game in the forest. He could have found something for himself. They couldn't afford to build a fire, though, and Kate couldn't eat fresh kill—wouldn't, he knew.

He wasn't about to tell her he'd nearly gotten his head shot off for stealing a picnic basket for her. He felt foolish enough as it was.

It made him angry all over again when he recalled arriving with his hard won trophy to find Kate's scent all over Silvair, and he with a self satisfied look upon his face.

He hadn't looked quite as pleased with himself after *he* had rearranged his face, Sergei thought with savage satisfaction.

"We don't have anything to put on this," Kate finally said, dismayed, feeling a little queasy at the thought that he'd almost gotten himself killed only for a little food. "You shouldn't have chanced it."

He shrugged, grinning wryly. "He was faster reloading dan I had expected."

Kate gaped at him. "Sergei! This is nothing to joke about! You're shot. You need a doctor."

"De bullet pass through."

"But ... it could get infected."

He frowned. "It won't. Dis is not your worry!"

Chastened, Kate sat back on her heels.

He cupped her chin in his palm, tipping her face up to study it and smiling faintly. "You are hungry? Let us see if what I stole is worth dis hole, *da*?"

Kate tried to return his cajoling smile, uncertain if the fluttering sensation in her belly was from the smile, his touch, or both, but discovering the appetite she'd had before had vanished.

Gathering up her clothes, she shook the dirt from them and put them on, wondering how she could feel so self-conscious dressing in front of him when she'd spent months stripping on a stage in front of hundreds of men.

There was a large thermos inside the basket filled with chilled sweet tea—the most welcome item in the basket as far as Kate was concerned. She filled the lid and drank it down while Sergei dug through the basket examining the other contents, unearthing cold chicken and potato salad, a variety of sandwiches—mostly peanut butter and jelly—and chips, and home baked cupcakes.

Some family was going home unhappy, Kate thought guiltily.

Sergei didn't seem to suffer any qualms about it. He helped himself to a piece of chicken and studied the potato salad before sniffing at it suspiciously.

Kate smiled faintly. "Never had potato salad, huh?"

There were no plates or eating utensils packed in the basket. Shrugging inwardly, Kate dug a finger into the plastic container he held and scooped up a small amount, offering it to him for a taste. He studied the offering quizzically a moment and then swooped to catch it in his mouth as it began to fall from her finger. Her chuckle at his quick save died as she felt his tongue swirl around her finger. When he closed his mouth on the digit and sucked it her belly quickened.

Abruptly self-conscience, she looked away as she reclaimed her finger, focusing on choosing a piece of chicken for herself. When she glanced at Sergei again it was in time to see him scoop a glob of potato salad into his mouth with his own finger. "Decided you liked it, huh?" she asked with a faint smile.

He rolled the food around in his mouth as if thinking it over and finally swallowed. "Tastes better wid your finger," he responded, a gleam of mischief in his eyes.

His teasing sent a pleasant flutter through her. God! It had been so long since a man had actually flirted with her! And how long since one as good looking as Sergei? Never?

The men at the club had talked to her—she supposed they'd considered it flirting, but 'hey baby, wanna sit on my face?' wasn't her idea of flirting.

"Dis Panas—why you was working for him?"

Kate sent him a quick glance and frowned. "It's a long story," she said reluctantly.

He shrugged, but his gaze was assessing. "We aren't going no wheres."

True, but she doubted he really wanted to hear it. Besides, it was sordid, and she doubted he'd believe her anyway. He seemed suspicious of her reluctance, though.

"This guy I was living with owed him money. We'd been together a little over a year, I guess, so I knew he had a problem with gambling. When he took off, I figured I was well rid of him—even though he took my cash when he left and everything I had that he could sell and get cash for.

"Anyway, I was still kicking myself for getting involved with him to start with, and congratulating myself over the fact that he'd at least had the grace to take off without putting me to the effort of kicking him out when Panas showed up looking for him."

She shuddered. "He got really ugly when he found out Jeff had skipped out on the money he owed, but he left and I figured he would go after Jeff and leave me alone."

She wrapped her arms around herself. "He did go after him—said Jeff had only managed to cough up a few hundred before he died and he figured I could work off Jeff's debt. I was scared to death of him—too scared to go to the cops. He'd told me he'd know if I tried it, and I was pretty convinced he would."

She shrugged. "I figured dancing in his club was better than the alternative and eventually I'd either get the debt paid off, or I'd get too old to dance and he'd let me go—or I'd figure out a way to get away from him."

He didn't comment on her tail of woe and she returned her

attention to her food with the reflection that she hadn't expected him to believe her anyway.

"Is a good ting I kill him, den," he ground out after a lengthy silence.

Kate shot a startled look at him. He'd suggested he had before. She wasn't happy that he'd come right out and admitted it to her.

He studied her face assessingly. "Whatever you tink, Kate, I won't hurt you. I kill Panas for what he done to me, but I tink maybe I shouldn't. Now, I tink he just needed killing. Dat kind of man-child, dey hurt too many peoples, and dey doan never stop till somebody kill dem."

His calm assessment sent a shiver down her spine, but she was obliged to admit he was right. Panas had admitted killing Jeff, but she'd overheard far more than that in the time she'd worked for him, or heard the other dancers talking about things *they* had overheard. He'd not only been a cold blooded murderer, he'd been very blasé about it, as if he had no fear at all about being caught.

And she supposed he had no reason to since he was perfectly willing to kill anybody who even thought about talking to the police about him.

She wasn't sorry to hear he was dead. She *was* sorry Sergei had admitted it to her because, whatever he said to the contrary, she knew he wasn't going to want to take the chance that she'd tell.

He shook his head at her. "You tink, now, dat every man is like Panas? I tell you because I doan want you to worry about dat man anymore."

She swallowed the food she'd been trying to eat with an effort. "I won't tell anyone."

He shrugged. "I go home now. De authorities here, dey don't find me. Dey could not prove dat I kill him anyway."

"Back to Russia, you mean?" she asked, and then could've bitten off her tongue. The stupidest thing she could do was to question him. The less she knew, the healthier it was for her. Her perceptions of both Sergei and Silvair, she knew, were seriously skewed. She didn't know if it was just an inability to maintain a high level of anxiety and fear—possibly due to the wear and tear of that much stress on her—or if she'd allowed herself to be lulled by the fact that neither man had been overtly threatening since they'd taken her, but she was becoming more and more inclined to think they *weren't* like Panas' bunch.

The sex, she knew, on their side, didn't necessarily mean a thing. From everything she'd learned about the Russian mobsters, they were capable of engaging in sex, torture, and murder with equal enthusiasm, in that order, and with the same woman, which meant Sergei and Silvair's enthusiasm for fucking her was a long way from a guarantee that she could trust them not to kill her when they were done.

She wasn't entirely certain of what to make of her own enthusiasm for them unless it was nothing more than a defense mechanism, just as her inclination to trust them was. Or maybe it was nothing more than a purely physical response to the right stimulus? Fear of death plus need to placate plus beautiful package and enthusiastic copulating equaled mind blowing climaxes?

He nodded, not, apparently, disturbed in the least by the question. "First I lose dem, den I find my way home. We are far from de sea here, da?"

The question surprised her. "A pretty good way, yes."

He nodded again, frowning. "You would help me get dere?"

"You're going to take a ship back?"

"Da. Ship bring me here. I go back same way."

She frowned. "Wouldn't a plane be faster?"

"A boat will be *better*," he said firmly. "I haf no papers."

She was all in favor of helping him in any way she could, especially since it seemed to her that his going meant she didn't have to worry about him having any concern about leaving a witness behind. She still didn't see how going by boat was going to eliminate the problem he had of having no papers, though.

"Silvair is going back home, too?" she asked tentatively.

His eyes narrowed, flicking over her face as if to gauge whether or not she was interested in Silvair staying. Finally, he shrugged. "We haf not discussed dis. But he does not belong here neider. He will want to go back, I am certain."

She couldn't help but wonder why either one of them had come to start with if they didn't 'belong' and were only interested in going back, but she certainly wasn't going to ask. She supposed, though, the encounter with Panas was enough to kill whatever enthusiasm they might have had for the US. And then, too, there was the need to escape the consequences of that encounter.

She couldn't help but wonder what had brought them to start with, though, and what it was that Panas had done that had precipitated the revenge.

In her old life, she hadn't known anybody who considered killing a solution to wrongs done to them, but these people were a breed apart from anyone she'd known then and that was like another lifetime or another world.

With perseverance, she managed to eat enough, she thought, to keep her strength up. She couldn't find a lot of enthusiasm for the food. Her stomach was still too knotted with anxiety, but she couldn't afford to let herself get weak from lack of food and liquids. It was easy to see Sergei and Silvair were going to be pushing hard to escape the net the authorities would be trying to throw up to catch them, which meant she was going to have to work hard to keep up. She might not get anything else for a while, she knew, and if the opportunity arose to escape Sergei and Silvair, she wanted to be able to seize it.

Sleep was another problem. It had taken a lot of effort to grow accustomed to working half the night and sleeping most of the day. She never really had, which was something that had been wearing her down for a long time, but she'd gotten used to it enough that, despite her fears, she'd conked out when the opportunity arose. For all that, she was pretty sure she hadn't managed to get more than a few hours sleep total.

When she'd finished eating, therefore, she got as comfortable as she could and tried to sleep. She dozed, but she didn't really sleep and when Silvair returned, she discovered they fully intended to push on even though it was dark by that time.

They abandoned the basket and used the fabric lining to bundle up the remaining food and the thermos into a makeshift backpack sort of thing. It was awkward carrying it slung over her shoulder but no clumsier, she supposed, than carrying the basket would've been.

She couldn't see worth a shit, though. She didn't know how it was that Sergei and Silvair seemed to manage without any trouble, but she stumbled along almost blind, tripping over small rocks and roots. Finally Sergei, with a sound of impatience, suggested they could make more progress carrying her. Silvair volunteered since Sergei had carried her earlier. Both of them ignored her insistence that she could walk just fine, and she found herself in the uncomfortable position of riding 'piggyback'.

She figured Silvair would get tired of it fairly quickly. If he did, he didn't say anything and once he'd settled her on his back, they began to move faster, almost loping through the darkness. It tired her just hanging on even though Silvair supported the bulk of her weight on his back, looping his arms around her legs to steady her.

After a few hours, exhaustion overtook her again. She dozed, her arms loosening until she started to slip. Rousing, she tightened her grip again, but in a few moments she was slipping again. Silvair finally stopped and allowed her to slip to the ground. After studying her for a few moments, Sergei pulled her shirt up, calmly removed her bra, and used it to bind her wrists together. Alarm went through her, but she was too tired to feel much and allowed herself to be convinced it was just to keep her from falling off. When he'd finished, he helped her onto his back, she settled her arms around his shoulders, and they started off again.

She managed to stay awake for a while, but even the threat inherent in having her wrists bound couldn't keep her awake. She drifted, dropped into nothingness, surfaced and dropped off again.

A bizarre dream took hold of her after a time. She dreamed Sergei had transformed into a cat. She *felt* the fur beneath her cheek, the sleek muscles that bunched and stretched beneath her. She was warm, though, relatively comfortable despite the jolting ride, or just too exhausted to rouse to full consciousness and the dream didn't disturb her enough to push her closer to full awareness even when it changed later and she dreamed she was lying on a bed of pine needles and grass, sandwiched between two great cats.

She was alone when she woke and so sore all over she couldn't think beyond the aches and pains immediately brought to her attention by the slight movements she'd made upon waking. Her arms, wrists, and shoulders hurt the worst, bringing to mind the fact that Sergei had tied her wrists together the night before. Dawn was breaking. She'd been tied up for hours, she knew, most of her weight suspended from her arms, which explained the aches. Prying her eyelids open, she examined her wrists. They were bruised, but no longer tied.

Pushing herself upright finally, she struggled to get her sluggish brain into gear, looking around. She was lying, she discovered, close to a narrow trickle of water that was barely enough to earn the name stream. Her muscles screamed in protest when she got to her feet and moved to it to splash water over her face and, since it at least appeared to be clear water, she rinsed her mouth, as well. She looked around then for enough shelter to answer the call of nature, stripping off her pants and shoes as she had before to keep from soiling them any more than they already were.

Returning to the stream afterwards, she stripped her shirt off and crouched naked by the water to take a stab at bathing herself the best she could before she dressed again. Turning her t-shirt inside out, she used it to dry off the best she could, but her skin was still damp as she struggled into her panties and jeans again and the damp t-shirt was *really* uncomfortable.

She was fully awake by the time she'd finished grooming the best she could, though, awake enough, finally, to realize that she hadn't seen a sign of either Sergei or Silvair since she'd woke up. Frowning, she surveyed the woods, cocking her head to listen when she didn't see them.

Had they left her, she wondered? Just gotten up while she

was sleeping and walked away?

She tried to calculate how long she'd been awake, but realized fairly quickly that that wasn't going to help her figure out how long they'd been gone—at least fifteen or twenty minutes, she knew, but they might've just gone off before she woke, or they could've been gone hours.

She discovered she had mixed feeling about it. It was an opportunity to escape with her life, but she couldn't dismiss the feeling of abandonment or the anxiety of discovering herself alone with no clear idea of how to get back to civilization.

Doing her best to ignore the downside to being alone, she glanced around for the bundle. Relieved when she found it lying in the grass where she'd awakened, she grabbed it up, slung it over her shoulder and glanced around, trying to decide which way to go. She couldn't actually see the sun, but she could tell the direction, she thought, where the most light was coming from. They'd been headed east, she knew, or thought she knew, since they'd left the club. She had no clear idea of how far they'd come, but she decided to head west anyway.

And, just in case they hadn't actually meant to leave her, but had gone off for some other reason expecting to find her where they'd left her, she moved as briskly as she could. She hadn't been walking more than ten minutes when she heard a rustle in the brush than sent a flurry of goosebumps over her and lifted the fine hairs on the back of her neck. It sounded loud—translation *big*! Her head whipped automatically toward the sound, her heart trying to leap from her chest.

At first, she couldn't see anything at all. Almost like a recognizable pattern emerging from an impressionistic painting, however, her eyes abruptly focused on one pattern that stood out.

A golden eye, and it was not attached to either of the men she'd spent the previous day with. The golden pattern of fur between black stripes was unmistakable.

She'd found the Siberian tiger ... or rather, he'd found her.

Chapter Eight

Somewhere in the back of Kate's mind, the warning shouted that running was the worst thing she could do, but her legs didn't get the message. Sucking in a sharp cry, she whirled and ran for all she was worth. Behind her, even above the frantic drumbeat of her blood in her ears, she heard the crashing and crackling of crushed brush as the thing bounded after her. The instinctive recognition of what the sounds meant pumped more adrenaline through her and her legs nearly outran her.

It was her inability to keep from throwing terrified glances over her shoulder to check to see just how close he was that became her downfall. In all likelihood, terror notwithstanding, logic would've told her there was no way in hell she was going to outrun the thing, but she would've tried until her heart failed her if she hadn't tripped over a root and sprawled out.

The tiger pounced on her the moment she slammed into the ground hard enough to knock the breath out of herself. Mindless panic still engulfed her. Instincts, not sentient thought, controlled her actions. She rolled beneath the great body, struggling to shove it away and find purchase to get to her feet again at the same time.

He pushed at her with one great paw. As light as the push was, she sprawled on her back and the moment she did, he sprawled on top of her, pinning her to the ground. She sucked in a terrified breath, her eyes nearly bulging from her head as she found herself face to face with the cat. His golden eyes seemed to drill through her as he stared back at her. After an agonizingly long moment, he dipped his head and nudged at her chin with his snout. Several more minutes, or maybe only seconds, passed before it finally sank into Kate's terrified mind that he was rubbing his face all over hers and nuzzling her neck, bumping gently—and he was purring, not growling, the rumbling, intermittent vibrations nearly deafening her.

A rash of goosebumps swept over her as he nudged her ear and flicked his tongue out and licked it. She squeezed her eyes closed, cringing in anticipation of sharp teeth piercing her skin. Instead, he went back to rubbing all over her.

She peeled one eyelid open a crack when he abruptly lifted his head and discovered that he had tensed with alertness and was staring at something beyond her view. He surged to his feet as suddenly as he'd lifted his head and then bounded away.

She lay where she was, too stunned to do anything else for several moments. The snap of a twig nearby brought her upright with a jerk, however, and she whirled toward the sound, expecting to see the tiger racing back to 'play' with his kill for a few more moments. Instead, she saw Silvair coming toward her.

Shoving herself to her feet, she ran to fling herself at him. He grunted when she plastered herself against him. The jolt rocked him, but he maintained his balance, wrapping his arms around her and holding her nearly as tightly as she was clinging to him. It was several moments before she realized he was shaking almost as much as she was. Confused, she pulled away to look up at him.

The discovery that he was shaking with suppressed mirth only added to her confusion, but it also sent a surge of resentment through her. She glared at him.

He shook his head, the amusement in his eyes lightening his expression until a faint smile dawned. "Dat vas foolish, Kate!" he said chidingly. "You should know never to run from a feline. It arouse de hunting instinct."

"I don't know what you find so damned funny about it!" she said resentfully.

"You look like gazelle bounding through de brush—very graceful, Katie."

She gave him a drop dead look. "Very funny, Silvair! I'm glad I was able to amuse you!"

He chuckled. "It gibe me de chance to stretch my legs, also, chasing you. Vhere you vas goin' in such a hurry, sveety?"

Kate looked away uncomfortably, pulling from his light

embrace and stepping away. "I was running from that tiger! I *told* you there was one running loose out here!"

He tilted his head, a knowing gleam in his golden eyes. "Before dat."

She didn't meet his gaze. "I was looking for you and Sergei," she lied. "Where is he by the way?"

"He circle round to head you off. You was goin' de wrong vay."

"Oh," Kate said, feeling her face redden as she glanced around. "I did tell you I had no sense of direction out here."

"Good ting ve run faster dan you den, ja?"

She ignored that provoking remark, having spied Sergei coming toward them through the brush. She couldn't tell by his expression, but he didn't look angry.

In fact, once he'd stopped and pinned her with his gaze, he looked downright amused. It seemed unavoidable that they'd thoroughly enjoyed chasing her. What she didn't understand was *why* they both seemed to have enjoyed it. She would've thought they'd be thoroughly pissed off at the necessity of doing so.

Not that she was knocking it!

"The tiger chased me," she told Sergei.

His lips quirked. "Did he?"

She frowned at him, interpreting the expression as amused disbelief. "There really was a tiger. Tell him, Silvair!"

Silvair chuckled. "Beeg tiger, ja! Ugly ting! Maybe we see dat handsome lion you tell us about, too, ja?"

Sergei glared at him.

There were tangible undercurrents between the two men, but Kate was damned if she could figure out what they were. "It was so odd!" she said thoughtfully. "He didn't even try to hurt me. He just … rubbed all over me and purred. Swear to god! He was purring!"

Sergei's expression lightened. "Maybe he like you, da?"

Kate reddened uncomfortably, instantly remembering her 'history' with the tiger. "You don't suppose he's gotten the idea he's … uh … mating with me?"

Silvair uttered a choked laugh, whereupon Sergei sent him a

fuming glare. "Maybe dat stoopid lion tink so," he growled, "but de tiger, he's very smart. He would not confuse a scrawny leedle man-child female for one of his tribe."

Kate and Silvair both glared at him.

"Maybe de tiger not too smart," Silvair retorted in a provoking purr of a voice. "Else he could see past his nose."

"Well! He was the one that …. Never mind," Kate finished hurriedly.

Sergei reddened and scowled at her.

"Maybe he isn't actually wild?" Kate speculated. "Or not completely? Panas said he'd been captured in the wild, but …."

"Or maybe you tame him, pretty Kate, ja?" Silvair suggested, his good humor returning as he took her arm and urged her to walk with him.

She glanced up at him and then at Sergei, who'd fallen into step on her other side. Sergei still looked mightily insulted. Kate frowned thoughtfully. "Truthfully, neither one of them seemed entirely wild. Of course, they were so tranqed up, poor things, I doubt they knew where they were. I'm almost sorry I let them go, now. I thought they'd be better off, but if they hurt anyone they'll be hunted down and killed. Even if they don't that's what'll probably happen if they're spotted.

"If I hadn't been so scared Panas would find out—and scared of them—where I wasn't thinking straight, I might have thought about calling the animal rights people. *Then*, they would probably have been ok.

"*That's* what I'll do," she said decisively. "When we get somewhere where I can get to a phone, I'll place an anonymous tip about them and they'll make sure they're recaptured and taken someplace where they'll be taken care of and no danger to themselves or others."

The two men exchanged a long look over her head.

She glanced from one to the other. "You don't think that's a good idea?"

"I tink you should forget about de cats. Dey take care ob demselves."

"But, I don't want them to get hurt!" Kate exclaimed in

dismay. "They don't belong here. If they did, I wouldn't worry about it, but they're completely out of their element."

"Maybe dey find dere vay home widout your help?" Silvair suggested soothingly.

"From here? Geography may not be my strong suit, but there's no way they can get home from here without someone taking them."

"Worry 'bout dat later," Sergei said with finality. "We have udder tings to tink about now."

Kate didn't doubt that they did, but she didn't especially want to think about the things she had on her plate. She was becoming less and less inclined to think they actually meant her any harm, but she didn't know if she could trust that belief. Right now, they seemed to think she might be useful to them. Sergei had asked her if she could get him to the coast. But it didn't necessarily follow that they wouldn't hurt her once she was no longer useful.

She was pretty sure she didn't want to trust her life to it, but she couldn't see any way out at the moment. She'd already tried twice to get away from them and although she appreciated the fact that neither one had seemed inclined to get mean and nasty about the attempts—the opposite, in point of fact—they were bound to get impatient if she continued to try.

She should at least pretend she was coming to trust them completely, she decided. Maybe that would lull them enough that they'd give her an opening to flee?

On the other hand, as long as it seemed safe to stay with them now, there didn't seem to be much point in trying anything, at all, until she was close to civilization. Otherwise, she was either going to die of exposure wandering around lost, or one of the cats would get her—or something else.

They kept a steady pace, but they didn't push her as they had the day before. She was still glad when they finally stopped sometime around midday near a small pool. Sergei scanned the area carefully through narrowed eyes. "We stay here a while and rest," he finally said, glancing at Silvair with lifted eyebrows.

Silvair nodded. "Is goot place."

Kate settled tiredly on a patch of low growing grasses and took her pack from her shoulder to examine the contents. When she glanced up again to ask them if they wanted any of the crushed sandwiches, she discovered that both men had removed their jeans and moved to the water's edge. Dropping the jeans on the muddy edge, they waded out until they were about knee deep and then dove in.

It was several moments before Kate came out of her trance and realized they'd disappeared under the water.

She hadn't adequately admired the pair, she mused, but then she hadn't seen them completely naked before—or from the back—muscular backs, taut buttocks, and well formed legs. The view was enough to make any woman's heart stop.

It was hard to say which man looked the best. Silvair was a bit leaner than Sergei, but just as sleekly muscular. Blond gods, she thought, wondering why she'd ever thought she had a 'thing' for tall, dark, and handsome.

She looked down at the sandwich she'd selected when they surfaced, struggling with the urge to join them. She needed a bath every bit as badly as they did, and wanted one just as bad. If she joined them, though, they were bound to think it was an invitation.

And there was something *wrong* with that?

It wasn't as if she'd played hard to get, or that there was any reason to, for that matter. She wasn't in *that* kind of situation and she certainly didn't regret bartering sex for life—even though she'd begun to wonder since if she'd even needed to. Somehow, she didn't think they would've treated her any differently if she'd ignored their desires.

They hadn't made her regret the decision to do so, for that matter. They'd not only been considerate of her needs, they hadn't demanded she lay down and spread her legs every time the notion struck them—hadn't instantly begun to act as if it was *their* pussy and she was only carrying it around for them.

Putting the food down uneaten, she stripped and carried her clothes to the water's edge. She wanted to be *completely* clean, if only for a little while. To her surprise, Sergei and Silvair both joined her after watching her work on her laundry for a few moments, scrubbing the jeans they'd been wearing. When Kate decided she'd done the best she could with what she had to work with—nothing but water and sand—she wrung as much water out of her clothes as she could and found a spot in the sun to spread them to dry. Wading out into the water again while Silvair and Sergei spread their jeans to dry, she ducked beneath the water and wet her hair, scrubbing at her scalp until her hair felt cleaner. She felt their attention, felt the rake of their gazes and knew they were studying her even as they went about bathing themselves, but neither man made any attempt to approach her or interrupt her bath.

She was almost disappointed.

Raking as many of the tangles from her hair as she could with her fingers, she squeezed as much of the water from it as she could and returned to her picnic. Silvair and Sergei joined her after a few minutes, but declined the sandwiches she offered. Instead, Sergei stretched out beside her and closed his eyes. Silvair settled a little further away, his back against a tree trunk. The next time she glanced his way, she saw that he, too, had closed his eyes.

Frowning thoughtfully, she finished her sandwich, wondering if they were actually asleep or feigning just to see what she would do. The temptation was high to test to see just how deeply they were sleeping, but she tamped it. She'd already decided it wasn't a good idea to try to elude them again, and certainly not when she'd only tried a few hours before. Finishing her sandwich, she drank the last of the tea and then found privacy for her needs. Silvair, she noticed, cracked one eye open to study her as she stepped behind the shrub. When she emerged a few minutes later, he closed his eye again. A faint smile curled his lips.

So much for their being sound asleep, she thought, moving down to the water again to wash herself. Tired, but not particularly sleepy, she settled near Sergei again, acutely conscious of the prickle of the brush beneath her butt and the air currents wafting across her bare skin.

She was almost *more* conscious of their nakedness and wondered that they seemed so completely relaxed and comfortable. An intangible something teased at the fringes of her mind as she flicked a glance over first one man and then the other. Typical of such things, the moment she pursued it, the 'something' slipped entirely from her grasp. Frowning thoughtfully, she plucked at the grass idly while she plucked at her mind, trying to shake the errant thought from her subconscious mind to the light of day. It annoyed her that it flitted at the edge of her mind, just out of reach.

It wasn't a memory, she finally decided. They reminded her of something. What that something was continued to evade her, though.

Giving up on that pursuit after several frustrating minutes, she shifted to find a more comfortable position. She wasn't particularly sleepy but finally decided to stretch out. No matter what position she tried, the light bothered her eyes, though, and she finally closed them, still working at the puzzle that was bothering her.

She was certain she didn't know either one of them, had never seen them before they'd grabbed her a few days earlier. Maybe they reminded her of someone else? Not in appearance. She dismissed that fairly quickly. She couldn't think of anyone during any period of her life that even remotely resembled either man. Physically, neither Sergei nor Silvair could hope to ever blend into any crowd and escape notice and it wasn't just their size or the fact that both wore their hair unfashionably long. The unusual color of their hair and eyes and skin tones set them apart as much as their height and the breath of shoulders and mass of well defined muscles. Their accents were as thick as pudding. Even though she was getting used to the way they pronounced their words, her brain still had a notable translation delay any time either one of them spoke, and she had a harder time with Silvair's accent than Sergei's.

It dawned on her abruptly that it was the way they carried themselves, held themselves, moved, that not only made them stand out from the 'herd', but it was also the 'something' that reminded her of something else. She examined the thought for several moments, but the sense that she'd hit upon at least part of what had been eluding her settled firmly in her mind.

She *still* couldn't figure out what it was that seemed familiar about it, though.

She decided after a while that it wasn't just the way they moved, though. It was attitude, a supreme self-confidence that bordered on arrogance—almost like—regalness, as if they were masters of all they surveyed, a true sense of superiority. As in, they didn't feel any need to make anyone else feel inferior to feel that way. It just came naturally and wasn't anything they thought about.

They hadn't given any appearance of fear, she realized, not at any time, not even when they'd fled before the hail of bullets Panas' men had sprayed at them. She hadn't realized that before because she'd been terrified out of her mind, but neither one of them had been in a mindless panic like she had. They'd exhibited a healthy dose of common sense and a great reluctance to have their hides filled with holes. They'd moved like greased lightning, evacuating the area with as much speed as possible, but they hadn't seemed scared or even anxious.

That, she realized, was why she hadn't continued to be afraid, either of pursuit or of them. *That* was what had lulled her into a sense of security, false or not. They were focused on the necessity of putting as much distance between themselves and possible pursuit as they could, but almost relaxed about it as if they were completely aware of the danger and yet didn't feel particularly threatened because they were absolutely certain they could handle it.

And because they were, *she* felt like they could handle it.

What was it about them, she wondered, that made them so certain they could handle whatever was thrown at them that they could stop in the middle of the day and simply sprawl out lazily in the sunlight and sleep like a couple of lazy cats?

A jolt went through her as that thought abruptly connected with the elusive 'something' that had been teasing at the back of her mind. Cats!

They reminded her of two huge cats; the way they moved, the 'don't give a damn' attitude, even the way they sprawled lazily when they settled to rest without any outward sign at all of alertness as if they didn't have a care in the world. And yet they were swift to react. In the blink of an eye they could go from completely relaxed to totally alert.

Strange, she thought, feeling her mind begin to drift toward sleep as soon as she stopped prodding it to unravel the mystery.

She drifted upward toward consciousness only a short while later, prodded there by invasive warmth from the hand lightly stroking her breasts and belly and the brush of bare skin along her back. For a moment, she wavered between annoyance and rising desire, then the pursuit of pleasure outstripped the urge to sink into oblivion again as she felt the heat of his rapid breaths caress her shoulder and then her neck. When his hand drifted down her belly and his finger parted the folds of flesh of her sex, stroking her damp cleft, she lost all interest in sleep. Shifting her leg to give him better access, she released a half moan, half sigh as he stroked her more deeply, pressing one thick finger inside of her.

He removed his finger after only a moment, pushing her onto her stomach, spreading her thighs with his and lifting her hips upward to give himself access to her body. His cock stretched the mouth of her sex, glided into her passage with the natural lubricant her body produced for him until her muscles strained against his girth and then slipped outward, returning more forcefully to conquer a few more inches of her channel, delving a little deeper each time until he was so deep she was panting with the fullness.

He settled against her, his chest brushing her back, his face burrowed against her neck so that his heated breath teased her skin. Shivers of delight skated over her at the feel of him against her, surrounding her, filling her with each thrust of his thick, hard flesh. A purring vibration issued from his chest as he increased the pace of his strokes. Her body quickened at the sound, at the pleasurable jolts that went through her at the glide of his flesh along her passage. Her entire being focused on that one point of exquisite contact. A low moan built in her chest as the sense of gathering grew inside of her and she knew with the next stroke, or the one after that, her body would explode with rapture. She focused on it, reached for it.

A powerful sense of deja vu` hit her from out of no where.

Her eyes flew wide for a split second, capturing the image of Silvair, watching them, his eyes slumberous with heated desire, and then her climax rocked her. She squeezed her eyes closed instinctively to savor the paroxysms of pleasure that went through her, one after another, building to a peak before she began to descend again.

Sergei uttered a choked grunt as his body seized, milked of his seed by the kneading contractions of her passage around his flesh. He lay more heavily against her in the aftermath, nuzzling his face against her hair and the side of her face, her shoulder, her neck. Through the darkness of her own sated bliss, dejavu` pierced her again, but it was as elusive as the first stab of recognition.

As Sergei rolled off of her at last, though, it hit her right between the eyes *why* it seemed so familiar.

Chapter Nine

Kate had barely caught her breath when Silvair pounced upon her. Scooping an arm beneath her belly, he lifted her hips until her knees were under her, positioned his body and drove inside of her. The force of his thrust punched the air from her lungs in a grunt. She wouldn't have thought, if she'd had time to think, that her body could yield up any more pleasure having just expended itself.

The fever of his need communicated itself to her body, however, resurrecting heat from the ashes of her climax. She climbed faster and further than before. Within moments she was gasping and moaning as her body quickened, tightened swiftly toward another release. It caught her unawares, hitting her with a blinding speed and force that tore a hoarse cry from her throat as it rocked her even as he drove so deeply inside of her she felt like he would split her in two and began to shudder and jerk with his own release.

Her entire body was sparking and jolting and smoldering as if she'd been hit by an electric current that fried every nerve ending as she came down. She collapsed weakly when he pulled free of her and released her, feeling as if she would melt into a puddle of boneless flesh.

Conscious, but barely, she drifted in the semi-darkness of supreme satisfaction, too weary to collect her thoughts, content to focus on breathing and nothing more for a while. It was only as her heart ceased to hammer in her chest and her lungs ceased to feel as if they couldn't gather enough oxygen that rational thought began to filter into her mind again. With thought came memory.

It was with a sense of shock that she realized she'd likened—her *mind* had linked--Sergei's coupling to one she'd tried damned hard to forget had ever happened.

Why in the world, she wondered, would she even *begin* to

compare what Sergei had just done to that bizarre attack by the tiger? True, he'd taken her from behind as the tiger had, engulfed her beneath his big body, nuzzled his face against her—but it certainly wasn't the first time she'd done it 'doggy'. Her ex had been fond of that position—*overly* fond to her mind. *She* didn't get anything out of it except sore knees and friction burn on her face if she wasn't damned careful.

She'd come, though, both when Sergei had pounded into her, and when Silvair had followed him.

And she'd come, much to her everlasting shame, when the tiger had taken her like that.

Thrusting that memory aside, unwilling to think about it, she struggled to roll over and finally sat up, pushing her hair out of her face. Sergei and Silvair were sprawled on either side of her, she discovered, eyeing each other with expressions that were a strange mixture of satisfaction and challenge.

The image of two huge cats eyeing one another and flicking their tails in displeasure rose in her mind. She banished it promptly, pushing to her feet and moving to the water to bathe herself. Her pussy complained at her touch, giving off renewed sparks of the pleasure she'd just experienced and reminding her, also, that she wasn't used to the activity she'd engaged in over the last couple of days—especially not the sexual activity.

She'd grown accustomed to frequent sex when she'd been living with Jeff naturally, but they'd parted company at least six month ago, she realized with a touch of surprise, maybe more. She'd been so miserable after Panas had grabbed her, she'd lost all sense of time.

She'd been assaulted both by Panas and several of his men in those first nightmarish months before she'd learned to evade their interest for the most part, but that had been rape, pure and simple and brutal. She'd done her best to block all of that from her mind and she sure as hell had never considered it sex, consensual or otherwise. It was humiliating, painful, degrading assault and not to be likened in any way with either lovemaking or healthy carnal pleasures. She'd hated every moment of it.

She had to wonder, though, if it had thoroughly fucked up her mind. She would certainly never have considered having sex with two men before her life had changed so radically, let alone enjoyed it so thoroughly. She sincerely doubted that she had managed to get her 'cookie' even half the time when she'd been with Jeff. They'd been fairly sexually compatible, but as with any long term relationship with a man that was totally self-centered, he'd had very little consideration for her wants or needs. He got pissed off when she didn't come, took it as a personal insult, but he didn't go out of his way to get her warmed up before he started and he didn't give a shit if she was in the mood or not. When he wanted it, he expected her to put out, right then, and enjoy it. A good half of the time, she'd just managed to get all warmed up when he finished, which so frustrated her she had a hard time trying to decide whether to let herself get 'in' to it, or just lay like a dead thing and let him have his way.

On the rare occasions when she was both in the mood and easily aroused, she came. The rest of the time she was either left behind or completely unmoved by the experience—except maybe annoyed at being bothered and left in a mess.

She didn't have that problem with either Sergei or Silvair, which was nice, actually, and still both puzzling and unnerving.

Maybe it was the danger?

The threat of death hadn't exactly turned her on before, though. If it was *that*, sex with Panas and his men should have totally blown her mind.

Dismissing it with an effort, she checked her clothes. They were still damp, but she decided to put them on again anyway. She still felt limp and wrung out from her romp with Silvair and Sergei. There was no sense in tempting fate—or them— by strolling around them naked.

She discovered with a touch of self-depreciating amusement that that wasn't going to be a problem. Sergei and Silvair had collected their jeans and put them on while she was bathing. She could tell by their expressions they weren't particularly happy or comfortable in the damp clothes. Neither was she, but at least her clothes smelled a little fresher.

Sergei surprised her when she'd gathered her little pack to go. Dragging her up against his length, he simply held her close for several moments, stroking her with his hands and nuzzling his face against her cheek and neck. He didn't kiss her. He sent Silvair a look that she could only interpret as challenging when he released her, which instantly blew the 'affection' theory that she'd been formulating out of the water.

She didn't miss the narrow eyed acknowledgment Silvair returned, either.

She certainly wasn't knocking all the stroking and nuzzling. It *felt* both appreciative and affectionate and she'd never had enough of either from any lover, up to and including those she'd spent several years living with. She just wasn't certain that was what it was. They always did that afterwards, she realized, both of them. How strange was it that they had such similar mannerisms when they hardly knew each other?

She couldn't even put it down to them being 'foreign' because they weren't from the same country.

And the other Russians she'd dealt with certainly hadn't been 'in' to appreciation. She was lucky if they didn't give her a kick on the way out.

She was inclined to just enjoy it. Whatever their reasons, she liked the way it made her feel—*not* as if she was just a handy hole on legs but like someone that actually mattered.

She knew she couldn't actually afford to allow herself to think like that, though. It was dangerous. Not being scared to death of them was one thing. Trusting them not to dispose of her when they were done was another thing altogether.

It flickered through her mind to wonder if they were interested in each other and just using her to annoy one another, but aside from that almost 'one upmanship' attitude she hadn't caught either one of them looking the other over with anything approaching sexual interest. They were clearly not homophobic, but she thought she could safely dismiss an interest in one another.

Particularly when she abruptly recalled that Sergei had gotten downright violent when he'd returned from his run to confuse their trail and discovered she'd had sex with Silvair while he was gone. She hadn't really thought about that at the time, but there didn't seem to be any other explanation for their fight.

And they'd definitely come to blows. Both Sergei and Silvair had been sporting some interesting bruises afterward—briefly.

It dawned on her that, despite the marks, they didn't actually look bruised today and she would've thought they would have. Even the bullet hole Sergei had had in his arm had closed and hardly looked like a wound now. With everything that had happened, she'd been too preoccupied to notice the wound. She would have, though, if he'd drawn her attention to it by favoring the arm in any way.

As strong and healthy as they looked, that still seemed like amazing healing powers. It puzzled her, but there didn't seem to be any other explanation for it—superior powers of healing, because they hadn't had anything at all to put on Sergei's wound to account for it and there wasn't actually a lot that could be done for bruises.

They moved with a purpose when they struck off again. She wasn't certain if that was because they *had* a purpose and/or destination in mind, or if it was because they'd moved completely out of the wooded area, which had become more and more sparse, and they were more exposed. A good bit of the state, the majority of it, actually, was semi-desert. She didn't recognize the area any better than she had the wooded region but figured they must still be in a section of the park they'd been traveling through. There wasn't a sign of any actual trees, but there was a good bit of scrubby growth that was nearly shoulder high to her. Both Sergei and Silvair were more exposed, being a good bit taller, and yet she couldn't help but notice they really didn't stand out that much. Their hair color and skin tones blended surprisingly well with their surroundings.

The terrain was flatter now that they'd descended from the foothills, but almost as hard to negotiate because of the thick brush and Kate was more than ready for a rest long before they finally stopped.

* * * *

Silvair slanted a speculative glance at Sergei who, like him, had sprawled beneath the debatable shade of a pine a short distance from Kate, who had settled to rest in the shade of another tree and dozed off. To all outward appearances, Sergei was dozing, as well, but Silvair was quite certain he wasn't, that he was, in fact, studying Kate, which was what he generally did when he was certain Kate was unaware of his interest.

"I am curious, my friend, to know vhat game dis is we play now," he murmured after a moment.

Sergei dragged his gaze from Kate, lifting one dark golden brow at Silvair, but he said nothing.

Frowning, Silvair studied the foliage he'd flattened to make a more comfortable spot to settle. "At first I thought it was only dat you vas being cautious, but ve travel for days now and ve both know ve covered our tracks vell. Several times now ve pass de trails dat lead to de villages of de man-children. De hunters are no doubt still anxious to capture de felines dey tink dey have been following, but dat is no problem for us since ve vent back and took care of de last of de bad men. De police vill not be looking for us in dis form. Dere is no one to tell dem and ve destroyed all de wideo tapes when ve destroyed de machines.

"You do not seem quite as anxious to return to your home as you vere to begin vith. And I do not tink you have decided dat dis climate agree wid you. It is much hotter here dan you are used to, ja?"

Sergei shrugged. "Nyet, I doan much care for de heat, but I grow accustomed. Dem was Russian mans dat ran dat place."

Silvair's lips thinned. "You tink to stay den? You lookin' dis place ober to find new territory? You doan have woman back dere?"

"Nyet," Sergei responded.

"Dis means no, ja? No to vich?"

Sergei sent him an assessing look. "Why you want to know?"

"I am curious," Silvair responded with a shrug. "Ve circle round and round, but go no vhere."

Sergei's eyes narrowed. "I go home when I am ready. You want to go now, go."

"I'm tinking I stay a vhile," Silvair said tightly. "I'm tinking I like dis place just fine."

"Dis place? Or Kate?"

Silvair slid a glance at Kate. "I'm tinking I like Kate just fine, too. She doan have no man. I doan have no mate."

Sergei glared at Silvair angrily. "She's a man-child. You can't take a man-child to mate—we can't breed our young on females of de tribe of man-children—even if she would agree and she wouldn't if she knew what you and I are."

"But you are happy enough to try," Silvair pointed out. "Dis is the de game, eh? You smell her time upon her, too. You tink you sew your seed enough it just might take, so we wander around dis place a while an' fuck de woman an' see?"

Sergei flushed. "Maybe I just like fuckin' de woman," he growled.

"Den why you try to mark her, eh?"

Sergei had nothing to say to that. He could have said it was unconscious, but he knew it wasn't and obviously Silvair knew it, too. *Why* he was doing it was the part that had been unconscious, the part he hadn't been willing to acknowledge to himself at any rate. He'd told himself he was in no hurry to go because there was no particular reason to rush now that they'd shaken the danger of being recaptured.

In the time since their escape, though, he'd begun to wonder just why he felt any need to return to his homeland. There was nothing for him there beyond the same miserable existence he'd known before and he'd acknowledged long before he was captured that it *was* miserable. He was perfectly content most of the time only to have his freedom, to roam the wilderness. There was comfort in the familiarity of it, of knowing every tree and path, every watering hole, even when times were hard in the deep winter and food scarce.

He had rarely worn his man-skin since he'd fled the villages of the man-children in his youth, but he was still man-beast, neither one nor the other, but both and, being both, he wasn't content to be completely alone. He might shake the need for companionship for long periods of time, but it was still there and there were times when the lack was nearly unbearable. He had not gotten used to it as the years passed. Instead, it had grown harder to bear.

"I have found no udders like me," he said finally. "I'm tinking, since I'm here already, dat I will look for udders before I decide if I will go back or not."

Silvair nodded. "Dere are many udders where I come from, but me, I'm tinking same ting. I will stay a while and see if dere are udders here. I like dis place fine. If dere are udders, den dere is no point in going back." He turned to study Kate. "Dis is not goot for Kate, though. As you say, she is man-child. Dis life is not for her. Even me, in man-skin, I doan do so goot. I'm tinking we need to take her back to her tribe. She will be better dere, and us, too, if we must stay in man-skin a while. An', if we find udders like us, den we will also learn where it is safe to shed de man-skin an' roam free."

Sergei felt his belly tighten and a wave of sickness roll through him. "She won't need us to take care ob her den," he agreed. "We gibe her some of dis money we take an' she will be good."

Silvair studied him from beneath slumberous eyelids. "She doan have no man-child tings no more. We smash her car. She got nowhere to work now, we kill de bad mans—goot ting for Kate, ja, but still no place to get de money now. I doan know if we take enough money to take care of Kate."

The comments brought a dark scowl to Sergie's face, not because he had any doubt that Silvair knew what he was talking about, or because he was reluctant to give her the money he had, or to get more for her if necessary, but because it occurred to him forcibly that he didn't like the way Kate had gotten money before. More accurately, he didn't like the thought of her dancing for the man-children. "Where we get more dis money, you tink?"

Silvair shrugged. "Same place man-children do, same way. We go to man-village and do man-child work. Me, I learn how to fix de cars man-children like, but I doan speak the man-speak speak here very goot. Could be a big problem, an' I doan have no papers neider. Could be a very big problem. You know how to do man-work?"

Sergei felt his face heat. "Ya," he said uncomfortably. "I make furniture—long time ago, though." A very long time, he thought wryly. The last time he'd tried to live among the man-children he'd discovered cabinet making had changed a good deal since his youth. They'd seemed far more interested in having him lift and carry things than using his hands to make furniture as his father had taught him. It hadn't mattered. He'd made enough money to live among them and that had been all he cared about because there'd seemed no reason to make more than necessary to take care of his needs. He would have to earn more than enough for his own needs, though, to take care of Kate. "I tink of something."

"We go back de udder vay, den," Silvair agreed. "Find a man-village. I doan tink we find one dis vay soon."

* * * *

Kate knew her knowledge of geography was seriously lacking, but, at first, she was more puzzled than suspicious when she noticed the terrain they were traversing was slowly changing from desert to brush to trees again. She was exhausted from the days of hiking, but it certainly didn't seem possible that they'd traveled far enough East to have left the desert behind. It wasn't until they stopped near dusk near a stream that looked damned familiar that she began to suspect they'd circled around, however, and were heading back in the direction from which they'd come.

She studied the stream and the surrounding area thoughtfully for a few moments, struggling with a sense of déjà vu and trying to decide whether to mention her suspicions or not and finally decided against it. She didn't think it was likely, despite their familiarity with the area, that Sergei or Silvair would've gotten lost. Either she was wrong, or they had a reason to circle.

They hadn't told *her*, but then she hadn't noticed any inclination in either of them to confide in her and she liked that just fine. She thought what she didn't know wasn't as likely to hurt her as knowing.

It still bothered her that she wasn't sure, and it also disturbed her that she *thought* they'd circled. It was hard to keep track of the days when she was so exhausted, but she was pretty sure they'd been hiking for a little over a week—maybe closer to two—and that still didn't seem nearly long enough that the manhunt would've been called off, or at least relocated to a different area.

Had they decided to take her back? And, if they had, was that a good thing? Or bad news?

Had she gotten too comfortable around them, she wondered in dismay? She was afraid that, maybe, she had. She hadn't even thought about trying to escape in days.

She'd realized the sense of lulling their suspicions before she tried it again and also the need to see either a sign of familiar terrain or some landmark that would tell her she must be close to civilization or at least an opportunity that would give her a fighting chance of actually succeeding in getting clean away.

None of that had transpired, and she was tempted just to excuse herself on that count, but she realized she hadn't really thought about escaping since, hadn't been all that watchful for an opportunity.

They'd lulled her into a sense of security, not the other way around, she realized with a flicker of dismay. She'd come to trust they wouldn't hurt her, and she knew she shouldn't. They hadn't hurt her or even threatened to. In point fact, it seemed to her that they'd gone out of their way to take care of her, but she knew enough about them to know it was still dangerously stupid to believe they'd have any compunction about killing her. They'd already killed, and they'd told her. They were on the run from both the cops and the Russian mob.

They might not *seem* like desperate men, but they had to be. They'd just relaxed because they hadn't encountered any threat since they'd escaped ... or at least mostly seemed that way— alert but not anxious.

"We rest here for a leedle while. I go find food," Sergei announced.

Kate's stomach growled at just the mention of food. She'd finished off the last of the stolen bounty that morning and hadn't had anything but a little water since.

She didn't know where he thought he was going to find food—unless he knew they were close to a place where he might get some—maybe a picnic area? Maybe he'd spotted a house, or a road?

She flicked a glance in his direction, but he hadn't waited around for any sort of comment. When she looked, he was already disappearing through the brush.

Trying to appear nonchalant, she moved to the stream and crouched to drink and wash her face and hands.

"I'm tinking we need fire," Silvair muttered. "I go find wood to burn."

Kate sent him a startled glance. They hadn't made a single fire in all the time she'd been with them. She'd assumed they didn't have the means to make one. They were being hunted, they knew, and she supposed they just hadn't thought it a good idea before now, but if they'd had the means wouldn't they at least have made a small fire?

Apparently not, she thought wryly.

And what could she make of the fact that they'd decided to now?

Just desperation for food? They had to be as hungry as she was. She couldn't help but notice that neither one of them had eaten much of the food Sergei had gotten before.

She got up when she'd finished drinking and found a place to relieve herself. Silvair had brought back a small armload of dead branches and was nursing a tiny fire when she returned. He motioned her over. "Dis keep de animals away. You get more sticks and feed, but doan make no beeg fire."

Kate stared at him, knowing he wouldn't have instructed her if he meant to stay. Her heart fluttered uncomfortably at the realization. Should she comment? Would it sound suspicious? Or would it sound more suspicious if she didn't?

He left while she was still trying to make up her mind.

Kate stared at the flames licking at the dry wood, trying to decide if she should seize the opportunity they'd given her. She lifted her head after a few minutes, staring around at the darkening landscape.

Maybe it was test?

What if he'd only gone a little ways and cut back to see what she would do?

What the hell would be the purpose of that?

Pushing to her feet, she frowned thoughtfully as she studied the ground in search of small branches to feed the fire, stopping to pick one up now and then.

She hadn't seen any sign of the cats in days. Did that mean they'd moved off? Or were they still roaming the area— maybe as hungry as she was because it was unfamiliar and there weren't a lot of big animals for them to feed on like there must be where they were from? Not that she knew a damned thing about the big cats, or the area they were from, but they *were* big. It was bound to take a lot of food to appease them.

A shiver skated through her. It took an effort to resist the urge to build the fire a little higher.

It was getting dark. Even if they were close to an area where she might stumble upon someone that could help her, it would *be* stumbling. She didn't know which direction to take except that she couldn't go off in the same direction as either Sergei or Silvair if she hoped to elude them.

The cats were probably night hunters.

With that thought, she abandoned the fire and began to search for firewood a little more desperately. She didn't want it to go out before Sergei or Silvair returned and she sure as hell didn't want to be blundering through the dark woods in search of wood.

She wandered farther from the fire than she'd realized. By the time she turned back with an armload of branches she thought would hold her until the men returned, she was at least fifty feet from it, and there was a very large mountain lion standing between her and fire.

Chapter Ten

Kate froze—heart, lungs, muscles, mind—staring at the huge animal unblinkingly.

He looked back at her with an unblinking stare.

She had a bad feeling he hadn't frozen in place for the same reason she had. She could see the tension in his great body, *knew* without a doubt that he would charge her if she moved in any direction.

Sergei, she discovered when she finally managed to unglue her eyeballs and flick a frantic glance around for an avenue of escape, had stepped from the woods behind the cat. He had frozen as she had, staring at the cat.

The cat didn't seem to sense his presence.

Kate swallowed convulsively, let out the breath she'd been holding very slowly, as if somewhere in her mind she feared the sound would be enough to set the beast in motion. When she flicked a frightened glance at Sergei again, she saw that Silvair had appeared beside him.

The mountain lion's ears twitched, rotated in search of a sound he'd undoubtedly heard. The fur along his back rippled. Blinking, he swiveled his head abruptly in the other direction. A low warning growl issued from his throat.

Kate sucked in a desperate breath of air and the cat's head jerked in her direction again.

It had marked her for dinner, she realized, and despite the presence of the men it wasn't ready to give up so easily.

It was trying to decide if it could get to her before they could attack, she realized as the cat turned to survey them again.

Either that or it was assessing the level of threat each of them represented.

It screamed abruptly, daring them, or warning them off, or maybe challenging them. She'd heard that, in the distance, the sound they made was almost like the scream of a woman. This close, it just sounded deadly, and she felt the fine hairs along her neck and the back of her head stand up. In slow motion, she stared at the thing as it abruptly surged into action, charging straight toward her.

Sergei and Silvair also leapt into action—leapt forward in a strange sort arch that looked almost like a dive. She blinked and as her eyelids slowly opened once more she saw the Siberian tiger and African lion where Sergei and Silvair had been only moments before. They roared a nearly simultaneous challenge as their forelegs struck the ground.

Kate couldn't have moved if she'd remembered she had legs. With wide, terrified eyes, she stared at the three huge cats charging toward her, sucked in a sharp, keening cry, and dropped the bundle of wood she'd been clutching to her as if it was some kind of shield.

The mountain lion skittered to a halt and whirled almost in the same motion. It's body quivered and rippled as it performed a strange little dance of indecision, obviously undecided whether to flee or fight. Just as clearly, it decided the two cats charging toward him were too close for a successful escape. Uttering another blood curdling scream, it lifted a paw, razor sharp claws extended, and swatted at the tiger, who was closest.

Time sped up from slow motion to fast forward. The snarls and roars of all three great cats were nearly deafening, but she could hear the meaty thuds of their blows, as well. The sounds, or the approach of the battle as the three cats tumbled and clawed and bit at each other, thawed Kate's frozen limbs. Screaming, with no idea at all of where she was running, she whirled away from the battle and fled.

Either it had grown too dark to see, or she was just blind with panic. It seemed she hit every tree and limb and fell over everything that littered the ground. She bounced from one to another, hit the dirt hard enough to knock the wind out of her, clawed her way upright and ran a few more feet before she collided with something else. The sounds of the battle dimmed behind her as did the glow from the fire, but she had no idea whether she'd put any significant distance between herself and the battle or if it was just her own rasping breaths and the thundering pound of her pulse in her ears that made it seem like she was making progress.

She reached a point where physical distress began to outweigh her terror, however, and as it did, her mind finally seemed to kick into gear. Her thoughts were still primal and basic, though, not rational, not clear cognition. 'Run' pounded through her mind until she reached the point where she knew she couldn't run any more without dropping dead. 'Climb' supplanted it when she'd exhausted the ability to run. She tried two trees before she managed to grasp a branch and haul herself up from the ground. She didn't stop until she reached a point where she couldn't find a limb to hold her weight.

Shaking all over, almost too weak to hold on as the adrenaline began to drain from her, she sat down on the branch she was standing on and coiled her arms and legs around the spindly tree trunk, pressing her face against the rough bark and squeezing her eyes closed. The tree swayed. Her belly clenched so hard she thought she might throw up for a moment.

"Kate! It is alright. Come down."

Kate unclenched her eyelids and peered down toward the ground below her. Dimly, she saw the shadowy figures of Sergei and Silvair. She stared at them hard, trying to decide whether she wanted to climb down or not.

The images from the clearing near the stream flickered through her mind like someone flipping a stack of still pictures in front of her face—Sergei, Silvair, the mountain lion, and then the tiger and the African lion and no Sergei, no Silvair. Try as she might, she couldn't summon any remembrance of seeing Sergei or Silvair after the tiger and the lion had appeared. They were there, then vanished, and the lion and tiger were there. "C ... ca ... cats?" she managed to stammer.

She saw the two glance at one another. "Ve have killed dat cat," Silvair said in what she figured was supposed to be a soothing assurance.

We?

She hadn't realized she was shaking so badly her teeth were

chattering. "Y-y-you?"

"Come down, Katie," Sergei said gruffly. "You know we will not hurt you."

She stared at him for a long moment and finally shook her head, though she wasn't certain if she was disputing his claim or just reluctant even to try to climb down. "N-no!"

"You vant me to climb up?" Silvair asked.

She stared down at him, trying to make out his expression, but it was useless. The shadows were too deep. "N-n-no."

"Den come down!" Sergei said imperiously.

She shook her head, tightening her grip on the trunk of the tree.

"You are not afraid of us, Katie?" Silvair asked coaxingly.

Was she? She couldn't decide if she was or not. "I s-s-saw. I s-s-saw …."

"Come down, Katie. We talk about dat, da?" Sergei said, his voice more placating now.

Talk about it? What she thought she'd seen? As hard as she'd been trying to convince herself that fear had fucked up her head, his comment seemed to dispute that more comforting explanation.

It could *not* have been real, though. She must have just focused on the cats when they'd come charging after the mountain lion and she hadn't been able to look beyond that. How had Sergei and Silvair killed the mountain lion, though? Silvair said *they* had killed it. Why would he say that?

Maybe he'd just meant that it was dead and she didn't have to worry anymore about it trying to eat her?

She took too long trying to make up her mind. They grew impatient. The shudder that went through the trunk she was clinging to shook her from her disjointed attempts to make any sense of what she'd seen—or what she thought she'd seen. Fear rippled through her. She tightened her grip and looked down to see that one of them was making his way up the tree.

It wasn't a very big tree. The higher he climbed, the stronger the sway. Kate thought she was going to loose control of her bladder as the damned tree began to swing back and forth. She realized it was Silvair climbing the tree about the time he reached a point where the tree, instead swaying, began to bend. The higher he climbed, the deeper the bend until she began to think the top would break off. It dipped until the top where she was perched was nearly horizontal to the ground. Feeling the shift in her weight, Kate gritted her teeth and clung with all her might, but she could feel her strength giving out.

She uttered a sharp scream as she lost her grip and plummeted toward the ground. It broke off abruptly as she landed in Sergei's outstretched arms. He merely broke her fall, however, slowing her descent but allowing her to slip to the ground. Her knees buckled as her feet made contact. His arms tightened. Her cheek slid down his stomach muscles. She wasn't certain if it was his grip that finally halted her slide or the fact that her chin hung in the waistband of his jeans.

He shifted his grip to her shoulders. Pulling her upright, he leaned down to peer at her face. Behind her, she heard a heavy thud as Silvair dropped to the ground and a jolt rippled all the way through her.

Apparently, Sergei saw something of her fear and shock in her face. After a moment, he straightened and pulled her snugly against his chest, holding her there by wrapping his long arms around her. She didn't try to struggle. She couldn't even think and she didn't want to. He felt warm and she was cold. His embrace felt protective and reassuring, and she needed that to banish the frightening images that kept fluttering at the back of her mind.

And she was too weak in the aftermath of her fright and flight to consider anything else.

When she didn't try to struggle and pull away, he leaned down, grasped her legs and lifted her completely off the ground. With her arms pinned by his hold, she couldn't do more than clutch at his sides, but as he began to carry her back toward their camp, she managed to disentangle one arm and hook it around his neck. Tightening her hold, she shifted upward enough to burrow her face against his neck.

He settled with her on his lap before the fire. She heard the crackle, felt the heat of it on her back, but the warmth emanating from him was more welcome, thawing her everywhere their bodies touched.   Eventually, the cold withdrew inside of her and the shivering dwindled to a shakiness that lingered at her core. The weakness became an irresistible lethargy that leadened her eyelids as he leached the cold from her.

He was still holding her when she woke up. She'd lost her grip on him when she dozed off, she supposed. She was still cradled against him, but she'd settled in the hollow formed by his folded legs, her back supported by one arm and her arm had slid down from his neck so that her palm was resting just above his heart.

Her awakening mind began to slowly sort through the images it had collected earlier, but the conclusion she drew from them was just as fantastic and unbelievable now as they had been at the height of her panic. She frowned with the effort to reason them away. Instead, more impressions flooded her mind to join them.

She'd dreamed while she'd dozed, she realized, dreamed of a hot, soothing tongue lathing the stinging scratches along her arms and hands, her neck and face. It had seemed real, and yet she realized it must have been inspired by the images planted in her mind before she'd dozed off.

The images that weren't real.

Sergei must have noticed she'd awakened. He transferred his gaze from the fire to her. His expression was unreadable, but she thought she saw a flicker of wariness in his eyes. "What happened?" she asked, her voice scratchy with sleep and maybe the emotions that began to well up from inside of her, as well.

Something flickered in his eyes. "De big cat decide he want to eat my tender leedle doe," he said with a hint of amusement.

Kate shuddered and struggled to sit up and look around the clearing. Silvair, she saw, was lounging on the other side of the fire, his gaze on her. The heavy darkness beyond the fire made it impossible to make anything out.

"He is gone," Silvair responded to her searching look, drawing her gaze back to him.

She frowned, trying to piece together the memories she'd

been so carefully shunning. "The tiger and the lion …."

She saw Silvair lift his gaze to Sergei and followed the look. Sergei met her gaze. "Dey kill de beeg cat."

Frowning as his comment prompted a memory, she looked away, struggling to capture it. Silvair caught her attention again as he sat up and reached to turn the spit she saw suspended over the fire. A row of small, slightly charred carcasses lined the spit—rabbits, she supposed—hoped. It wasn't the mountain lion, she realized with a sense of relief, but she still felt vaguely nauseated.

"I'm tinking dis is cooked. You hungry, Katie?"

She was more than a little revolted at the thought when she'd come so close to being dinner herself. They'd gone to a lot of trouble, she didn't doubt, to get the food, though, and clean and skin it.

She wondered abruptly how they'd managed it when she hadn't seen either one of them with even a knife. She dismissed it after a moment and forced an expression of interest. "A little," she managed to say.

She didn't want to move away from Sergei, but it dawned on her he must be awfully uncomfortable after holding her so long. Besides, he wouldn't be able to eat with her perched on his lap. He helped her when she struggled to get up. She noticed he flexed his arms and legs when she'd moved to settle between him and Silvair, but he didn't say anything.

She also noticed he had faint red furrows along his cheek, his chest, and what looked like puncture wounds on his upper arm and shoulder. She stared at the marks, but she knew they hadn't been there before. It didn't look like scratches from briars or brush. The marks were regularly spaced—like claw marks and teeth marks.

It couldn't be that. If the cat had clawed him, it would have filleted his flesh, not just left the angry red furrows, and if it had bitten him, it would've torn out a chunk of flesh.

Silvair had similar marks on him she discovered when she turned to study him as he pulled the spit from the fire and settled it on a row of smooth rocks for the meat to cool.

"How did you get scratched up?" she asked abruptly.

Both men tensed, but they didn't look at each other.

"Dem rabbits, dey put up a hell of a fight," Silvair said after a moment.

Kate was not amused.

"We heard de beeg cat," Sergei said. "We run tru de brush."

Kate frowned, summoning the memory. That one was actually pretty clear. Sergei had stepped from the woods and then Silvair, and neither one of them looked as if they'd been running. Besides, the cat hadn't made a sound—didn't until just moments before it attacked. "You said you and Sergei killed it," she said slowly.

"Dem beeg cats you saw kill it," Sergei said easily.

Kate shook her head. "No, before that, when I was in the tree—Silvair said you two had killed it."

Sergei shrugged easily. "It sound good. De man-child eater, he's dead. Dat's a good ting. Doan matter how, does it?"

Kate frowned, struggling again with the bizarre image that flooded her mind. Sergei and Silvair had launched themselves at the mountain lion as it had charged her, but they hadn't *run* toward it as she would've thought, they'd ... sprung. Was that why her mind kept superimposing images of the cats over them? Because they'd moved like cats rather than men?

Why would they move like cats instead of men?

Silvair tore off a hind quarter of one of the rabbits and held it out to her. She stared at it a moment before she took it. The meat was still hot and she juggled it for several moments until it cooled enough to hold it.

Picking at it absently, she rolled the thoughts around in her head. "Why did you call it a man-child eater?"

Sergei frowned. "You tink he confuse you wid a doe?" he said finally. "Dat cat, he know you are a man-child. He stalk because he doan fear man-child, *know* de man-child is easy prey."

A shiver skated through her, but she dismissed the quivering in her belly. "Why do keep calling me a man-child, though?"

He exchanged an uncomfortable glance with Silvair, seemed to think it over. "My English bad, very bad. What would you call it?"

Kate eyed him doubtfully. It was true his accent was thick, and his English pretty broken, but he had a fair vocabulary for all that—both of them did—and she didn't think that was why they kept referring to her as a man-child. They always had, she recalled, and she'd thought it was strange to begin with. She hadn't realized before, though, that it was as if they were separating themselves from her and the other 'man-children'.

She ignored his attempt—and she knew that was what it was—to divert her. "You don't think of yourselves as man-children, though."

Silvair sighed and sat up.

Sergei sent him a hard look. "Don't," he growled.

Silvair met his gaze. "She saw. She doan want to accept, but she saw."

Kate felt her belly quiver. "I didn't imagine it, did I?" she demanded shakily.

"Dis is against de laws of de people," Sergei said warningly, ignoring her question, his gaze still boring into Silvair.

Silvair met his stare for a long moment and finally shrugged. "Eat, Katie. Den we rest. Den we take you to the village of de man-child."

That announcement diverted her. "Town? You're taking me back to town?" she gasped.

"Dis place not goot for you, Katie, even widout de bad cat."

"But ... Panas and his men."

"Those bad mans dead, too. Dey woan hurt you now, Katie," Sergei said soothingly.

She stared at them in dismay, realizing they had no idea what she'd be facing when she went back.

They didn't because they didn't really understand the world of the man-child—because they weren't man-children.

Chapter Eleven

Kate felt oddly detached from the thoughts rambling around in her mind. Slowly, mechanically, she chewed and swallowed her food, but she was only peripherally aware of the taste and texture, little more aware of it than she was the emotions she seemed walled off from feeling. A small part of her was concerned about the detachment, but she was content enough with it not to feel a need to breach the wall.

When she'd finished eating, she went through her nightly ritual of settling without any need for actual focus on it— bathing in the stream, leaving to relieve herself, and then returning to curl on her side to sleep. One of them had doused the fire once the food was cooked, but it still gave off warmth and she settled near it.

Leaving off her examination of recent events, she went back to the beginning, when they'd first fled the club, and examined everything that had happened with new eyes.

They looked human. She'd accepted that they were, and she'd still thought they had strange mannerisms. She might not have noticed if it had only been one of them. The fact that they behaved so oddly, and yet very much alike, had struck her as peculiar to begin with, though, when there was no logical reason why they should. They weren't related. They didn't even know each other. They were from different parts of the globe.

And yet they both had the odd habit of rubbing all over her.

She'd even thought they reminded her of great cats the way they moved, the way they lounged lazily in the sun as if they didn't have a care in the world, appearing to be asleep or half-asleep. Yet, with the slightest sound, their eyes opened and they were clearly completely alert. They even had a way of lifting their heads as if they were sniffing the air.

She'd seen them change from human to great cat.

They didn't claim to be human because they weren't. They weren't even humans with the ability to shift into animals, she realized. They were felines with the ability to shift into humans.

Was she to accept what she'd seen with her own eyes, a fact borne up by the observations she'd made before? Or what she'd been told to believe was possible?

She realized it wasn't really a question of whether she *should* believe or not. She *did* believe it.

Sergei settled behind her. Curling around her body, he nuzzled his face against her neck and finally pulled her over to lie on her back. She stared up at him with a faint sense of uneasiness. He studied her face for a long moment and finally lowered his head to cover her mouth with his. The wall of detachment crumbled with the first touch of his lips to hers. She tensed as images of the Siberian tiger filled her mind, and then Sergei's heat and taste flooded her senses. Heady pleasure infiltrated her entire being. Her mind whirled in the vortex it created. Heat flashed along every nerve ending and melted her reserve.

She sucked in a shaky breath when he lifted his lips from hers and explored her throat. The hand he skimmed beneath her shirt to cup and knead her breasts trembled with eagerness. His need fed hers. She was panting for breath by the time he followed the path of his hands with his mouth and began to suckle and tug at her nipples with an eagerness that sent electric jolts through her and beaded her skin all over with sensation. Heated moisture flooded her nether regions. Cradling his head to her breasts, she arched her hips against him in a rhythmic pressure she was scarcely aware of until he pulled away from her abruptly and sat up.

She shivered at the cool air that wafted over her damp nipples, causing them to tighten into a harder knot, but anticipation rose to a higher level as he grasped the fastening of her jeans and tore at them. Jerking them from her, he tossed her clothing aside, pushed her legs wide, and fell over her. Catching his weight on his elbows, he undulated his body against hers, skin to skin, jeans to skin, knit to skin, rubbing his big body along hers as he nuzzled his face against hers and her throat, nipping and sucking and licking her. The variation of textures from his jeans and her blouse, still twisted above her breasts, teased her with each movement. She chafed at the impediment, wanting to feel nothing between them at all and yet it seemed to magnify the sensations every where their skin touched.

She stroked her hands along his shoulders, digging her fingers into his flesh to encourage him and when that didn't seem to be enough she gasped his name. "Sergei, come inside me," she whispered feverishly.

A shiver rippled along his length. He thrust his hand between them. Tugging at his jeans until he could shove them down his hips, he shifted upward to spear her with the head of his cock. She groaned with a mixture of bliss and impatience when he impaled her, drove just deeply enough inside of her to make her ache for more. When he lifted his hips to withdraw and push again, she opened her legs wider, curled her hips to receive him, and reached down to cup his buttocks. He released a rumbling growl as he plowed into her again, pushing relentlessly until he'd forced his hard flesh as deeply inside of her as he could go.

She wanted to hold him there just to relish the depth of their connection. As he began to pump in and out of her with more feverish need than finesse, though, and the stroke of his hard flesh along her channel sent out waves of delicious sensation, the pulsing need to feel that overshadowed the first urge. She moved with him, driving her body onto his shaft with a fervor that matched his until she reached the pinnacle, exploding in a fiery ball of ecstasy as she felt his cock jerk inside of her, heard the breathless grunts pulled from him as his body expelled his seed.

He lay heavily against her for some moments, his body still wracked with an occasional shudder. A beatific lassitude had filled her as her rapture abated. Disappointment invaded it briefly as he shifted downward to disengage their bodies, but he leavened it by nuzzling his face against hers for a moment before he moved off of her.

He'd already grasped her to drag her closer when Silvair settled beside her and planted his hand possessively along her waist. A low warning growl issued from both men's chests as they stared at one another across her.

The threat made the hairs on her neck prickle, piercing her contentment. Unnerved by their hostility, she struggled to sit up. For a moment more, they glared at one another, and then Silvair thrust his fingers in her hair and dragged her close. The hunger of his kiss shot through her like a potent drug, reheating the dimming warmth from her climax. Her flesh, still sensitive from the stimulation of before, responded to his touch with nearly painful pleasure as he pressed her back against the ground and stroked his hand over her in a restless quest to explore her thoroughly.

He broke the kiss after only a few moments, blazing a trail down her throat and continued along the center of her body, nipping at her with lips and teeth until he reached her lower belly before he moved up again and teased first one breast and then the other. The jolts that went through her as he suckled her nipples were almost painful in intensity.

She moved beyond dizzy to faint, her gasps rapidly escalating from moans to whimpers as his heat scorched her. "Silvair! Now! Please!" she gasped finally.

A shudder traveled through him. He covered her mouth again in a torrid kiss as he reached between them to thrust his jeans out of his way. She uttered a choked gasp as he aligned his flesh with hers and drove into her, seating his shaft deeply inside of her despite the clinging walls of her passage in a handful of desperate strokes. The first quaking of imminent release spiraled through almost at once. She clung to him desperately, tipping her hips to feel his pounding thrusts where she needed it most, to quell the throbbing ache. Her second climax hit her harder than the first, dragging a sharp cry from her lips in spite of her efforts to contain it. She bucked against him, shuddering as the quakes ripped through her, clinging tightly to him in the aftermath until she felt him reach his own crises.

Oblivion swallowed her up even as she heard him grinding

his teeth as his body convulsed with rapture.

* * * *

Kate's first thought as she woke was the answer to something that had teased her dreams. He had been waiting for her to beg him, she thought as she surfaced toward consciousness, recalling that Silvair had teased her until she'd thought she couldn't stand it anymore before he'd finally claimed her.

Because she'd begged Sergei and he was determined to have nothing less?

Rivalry.

The thought, the memory, evoked a ripple of shivers through her.

There was no doubt in her mind that he'd been needy. Neither one of them had demanded sex in days and she hadn't known what to make of that beyond being uneasy that maybe they'd lost interest in their 'plaything'. Considering their enthusiasm to start with she didn't think she could put it down to the possibility that they'd satisfied their sexual appetite, which hadn't left her with any other explanation, and it had begun to worry her that they'd lost interest in the only use they had for her.

Her reaction disturbed her more than a little. Not only had she had plenty of sex to take care of her personal needs to make her reaction the night before a tad excessive, but she thought the incident with the mountain lion and her discovery should have killed *any* enthusiasm.

On the other hand, as convinced as she'd been, or thought she had been, that she'd stumbled upon something she'd heretofore considered didn't exist, couldn't possibly exist, doubts had resurfaced with the morning light.

Maybe she wasn't as certain then as she'd thought? And maybe relief accounted for the sense of desperation she'd felt, relief that she'd survived the attack by the mountain lion and relief that she'd been wrong thinking they didn't have any use for her anymore?

She wasn't completely satisfied with those answers. She set them aside and got up to make ready to leave, though, when

Silvair and Sergei, who'd slept on either side of her like bookends throughout the night, got up. Sergei produced the leftovers from their meal the night before when she returned from the woods, which made her stomach lurch even though she was surprised and even grateful for his thoughtfulness, especially since she'd thought they'd gotten rid of what hadn't been eaten. She wasn't much for food immediately after waking, though, not at the best of times and not with food she *really* liked. It took all she could do to swallow even a little of the cold rabbit.

She was awake enough by the time she had to realize that they'd actually slept the entire night. It was the first time since they'd fled that they'd stopped for more than a few hours. "You think they've stopped looking for us?" she asked tentatively.

Sergei, who was busy eliminating the signs of the small fire they'd built, tilted a speculative look at her. "No," he replied finally. "They are still looking."

She blushed, realizing how stupid it sounded that the cops would give up a manhunt after what must have happened at the club. "But we're a long way from the search now, huh?"

He grunted, shoving to his feet.

She supposed that was a yes considering they'd stopped to hunt the night before, built a fire, and lingered to rest all night—which she could've figured out herself.

She'd been looking for some kind of reassurance. "We're going into town so we can get a car—or figure out some way to make it to the coast?"

Sergei and Silvair exchanged a look. "We take you to town, den we see, da," Sergei responded.

She really didn't think it was a good idea to go into town—*any* town—so soon after the incident, but she didn't think she was going to have much luck convincing them of that. It was their show. She was just along for the ride.

"We need to figure out some way to do something about our appearance if we don't want to attract too much attention," she said, pursuing it anyway.

The two men looked each other over critically and then

studied her. "We find clothes," Silvair said decisively.

"We can't just *take* clothes from somewhere," Kate said uncomfortably. "If the cops are looking for us and they hear about it …. I don't think I'd look too suspicious. Well, I suppose I look like a bag lady, but nobody pays them too much attention. I could find a secondhand shop and get what we need … if you'd trust me to do that. Without shirts or shoes you two would look very conspicuous."

Neither one of them commented on the suggestion, but they looked thoughtful and she decided to leave it at that. If she tried too hard to convince them they might become more suspicious instead of more convinced.

She didn't know if they had reason to distrust her or not. She'd meant it when she'd made the suggestion. It wasn't until afterward that it had occurred to her that it would give her a chance to escape. Reluctance immediately followed the thought, but she realized when she'd thought it over that she would be better off if she didn't betray any tentative trust at this stage. They'd still be close, too close for comfort.

It seemed to her that they didn't really mean her any harm, mostly because they didn't seem to see her as a threat to them regardless of what she knew, and that they had every intention of moving on as quickly as they could. Wouldn't it be better, if they weren't actually a threat at this point, to help them? She certainly wouldn't have to worry about either of them if she helped them get on a boat bound for the other side of the globe.

That was assuming the police hadn't actually managed to identify them. The cops would know about her, though, and they'd be looking for her—as an accessory or a victim. Either way it was going to be bad news for her.

She hadn't had time to consider what she was going to do if they actually let her go, she realized in dismay. She'd been too focused on surviving to consider she wouldn't be safe even if she did manage to elude them, or they let her go.

Should she *go* to the cops and try to worm her way out of this situation? Try to hide from them?

She wasn't going to the cops, she decided. She only had Sergei and Silvair's assurance that Panas was no longer a threat to her. She believed them—as far as that went—but that didn't mean the mob wasn't a threat to her and it didn't mean none of Panas goons were a threat.

Going to the cops would just get her killed.

She was reluctant to do so anyway. In the first place, she didn't know that she could convince them she'd had nothing to do with the business at the club, particularly since she was pretty sure she had. In the second, whether they'd intended to or not, Sergei and Silvair had done her a favor by freeing her from Panas, and it didn't feel right to point the finger at them, even if she thought they were safely beyond the reach of U.S. laws.

She was going to have to figure out what she could do to save her own ass if she managed to help Sergei and Silvair escape.

The first thing that came to mind was hitting for home, which was bizarre since she hadn't considered going home since she'd 'escaped' years ago. It probably wasn't a good idea anyway. One of the reasons she'd left to begin with was because her home town was so tiny it was stifling. Everyone not only knew everyone else, they knew their business. If she popped up again, even after so many years, *especially* after so many years, they'd start digging.

There was no one to go back to anyway. Her grandparents, who'd raised her, were dead, the people she'd considered friends scattered to the four winds. She didn't *want* to go back. It was a community with 'old fashioned values' and they'd always looked down their noses at her because her mother had returned from the 'big city' pregnant and unwed—compounding her sin by producing twins. Her fraternal twin, a brother, had died of crib death before he was six months old, though, and two years later her mother, pregnant with twins again and with no man in sight to claim them, had 'accidentally' OD'd trying to self-abort, which had effectively removed her from their spite and left her daughter to bear the brunt of it.

Part of the idea had some merit, though, she decided. Dirtville off-the-map USA was probably a better place to go than another city. She could find some kind work to survive and lay low. Eventually, maybe, they'd stop looking for her and she could have a 'real' life again, but the truth was she hadn't in so long, and hadn't thought she had a future at all, that she'd grown accustomed to just surviving. Living without a daily threat would be a huge improvement over what she'd had since Panas had come into her life. She'd long since given up the idea of a career, or anything approaching the American dream.

If she could just stay out of jail, and the cemetery, she thought she'd be content with whatever she could manage.

All she had to figure out was how to get there when she had no money and no identification and didn't dare go back to her place.

* * * *

They found themselves on the outskirts of a city the following day just after dusk. Kate had no idea what city except that it wasn't the one where she'd been living the past several years and that was enough to make her feel considerably better about proceeding.

Undoubtedly, they'd traveled much further than she'd thought they had.

Trying to be as unobtrusive as possible, they kept to the shadows and kept moving until they'd found themselves in the more unsavory area of the city, where they stuck out less from the local wildlife. They still gathered stares, which didn't surprise Kate in the least. Neither Sergei nor Silvair would ever have simply blended in anywhere except on a movie set or maybe at a weightlifter's convention. They were too remarkable in every way. Shirtless, barefoot, and built like two bouncers on steroids, even in an area where most people tended to mind their own business, people stared.

The motel Kate finally decided to try looked like one whose customers generally paid by the hour. She didn't like the idea of staying there, but she knew they didn't have a chance in hell of getting a room at a decent motel. This one at least would give them a little privacy since it was built in the style of the old motor courts with separate cabins.

It wasn't reassuring that she had to register and pay through a small security window either, but beyond giving her one piercing glance, the manager didn't indicate any particular curiosity or suspicion when she paid cash. The price was outrageous considering what a dump the place was, but Kate knew better than to object. She paid with the money Sergei had given her, took the key, and asked for clean linens.

She had to pay extra for bed linens, but she didn't trust that the bed had been changed since the last occupant and she wasn't about to sleep on a bed she was certain was working alive with germs, if not larger vermin, and god only knew how many varied body fluids.

Sergei and Silvair slid out of the shadows as she left the office and headed toward the cabin they'd rented. Without surprise, Kate discovered the room was horrible. It didn't look as if it had ever actually been cleaned. The carpet was an indiscriminate shade of brown/gold, antiquated shag that had no doubt been on the floor since shag was a fad, with blotchy stains she couldn't have identified if she'd wanted to.

Sergei and Silvair almost reeled away as she opened the door to the musty room. Looking as disgusted as she felt, they prowled the room, staring at the stained carpet, the sticky surfaces of the broken down, Danish modern particle board furnishings that masqueraded as wood, the ancient TV set on the dresser, the faded pictures hanging on the peeling wallpapered walls, the rickety table and chair set in one corner, and the lumpy bed. The air, besides reeking with unpleasant odors, was as damp and sticky as the furniture.

Kate didn't even want to set her clean linens down for fear the room would taint them before she could replace what was on the bed. "At least it's a room," she said into the dead silence, trying to sound cheerful.

Both men turned to look at her. Sergei's expression was dubious. Silvair just looked disgusted. "Dis place is not fit for dogs," Silvair muttered.

The comment seemed to amuse Sergei, briefly. "Dogs! Bah! Dogs would not want to stay in dis place. We pay to stay in dis place?" Sergei growled. "Dat man should pay us to stay."

Uncomfortably aware that she was the one that had chosen it, Kate shrugged. "It's just for the one night. I can get us some clothes tomorrow and we won't have to worry so much about drawing unwanted attention to ourselves."

Neither man looked terribly appeased by the suggestion.

"At least we can get a real bath—with soap and hot water. And sleep on a bed instead of the hard ground."

Sergei turned to study the bed. "I'm tinking de ground better dan dat ting." He shrugged. "You like dis place, Katie?" he asked doubtfully.

Kate gave him a wry look. "No, but I didn't think it was safe to try any place that wasn't sleazy. We *look* like fugitives from the law. It won't be so bad if we open the windows and let it air out some. And I got clean sheets for the bed and clean towels."

The windows were either nailed shut or painted shut—painted, she decided when Sergei opened one anyway, exerting more strength when it didn't open at his first effort and slamming the window up so hard it broke the wood and cracked three of the panes. As soon as he let go of it, it crashed downward again, and a chunk of the cracked glass parted company with the window and hit the floor.

Kate gaped at the window in horror.

Sergei glared at it when he discovered it wouldn't stay up and, after glancing around, jerked the drawer out of the bedside table and shoved it under the window to hold it up.

The sound of splintering wood and breaking glass drew her into the bathroom. Silvair was peering out of the hole where the window had been. He glanced at her and shrugged. "It fall out."

Stunned, Kate stared at the broken pieces of window molding for a moment and finally moved to the wall to peer outside herself. The window, which had once held frosted glass panes, was lying in a heap of splintered glass on the ground outside. "I don't think this was designed to open," she murmured.

"Dis is better," Silvair announced. "De air carry away some

of de stink of dis place."

"Good point," Kate murmured unhappily, hoping no one had heard or would feel inclined to call the manager if they had, "we've got a nice cross draft now."

Nodding, Silvair moved to examine the shower.

Tense already, Kate nearly jumped out of her skin when she heard the TV blare. Static filled the air. Heavy thumps punctuated it, and Kate dashed back into the main room to stop Sergei before he broke the TV, as well. "I think it's probably broke ... now," Kate said quickly, edging Sergei out of the way and flipping the channel. A grainy picture emerged to her surprise. "Hey! It works—sort of." She moved across the room, narrowing her eyes. "You can make out the picture from here."

Lifting his thick blond brows doubtfully, Sergei followed her and turned to study the TV again. While he was preoccupied with the TV and Silvair was entertaining himself taking the bathroom apart, Kate moved to the bed, grabbed the bedspread with one hand and dragged it off onto the floor. Making a mental note to wash that hand thoroughly with soap and scalding water when she'd finished, she dragged the sheets off behind it.

The mattress looked pretty horrible. Closing her mind to any interpretation of the stains, she dragged one of the clean sheets from beneath her arm and shook it open. Both sheets, she discovered, were flats—and thin enough she was pretty sure she could read a newspaper through them. Trying not to think about germs crawling through the open weave of the fabric, she made the bed. When she'd finished, she discovered Sergei and Silvair and sprawled in the two rickety straight chairs the room boasted.

She was surprised both chairs hadn't promptly collapsed beneath their weight. Obviously, they were better constructed than they looked. "If you two don't object, I think I'll take a shower and then I'll go out and pick up something for us to eat, if you like."

They exchanged a look, but neither of them said anything. Taking that as a yes, she left them staring at the TV and went in to take the first decent bath she'd had in a week and a half of running. Her hopes of having a hot bath, unfortunately, were doomed. The water never got above tepid, but at that it was still better than the cold streams she'd been bathing in and she had soap and a wash cloth.

The 'amenities' included a tiny bottle of shampoo, which didn't smell a lot better than the cheap soap, but was still better than nothing.

The black, windowless aperture unnerved her. As small as it was, she was sure a man could still climb through it and it wasn't the sort of neighborhood where a person could feel safe without a barred door.

She hated to put her dirty clothes back on when she'd finished bathing, but she didn't have a choice. She couldn't stroll down the street naked to get them something to eat.

When she returned at last to the main room, she discovered it hadn't been necessary. Sergei was gone. "Where's Sergei?"

Silvair shrugged without concern. "He vent to find food."

Chapter Twelve

The sound of sirens woke Kate from a deep sleep. Stirring, she reached out for the warmth of Silvair's form and discovered the side of the bed empty. Rolling over in search of Sergei, who'd been lying behind her when she dozed off, she discovered that he was gone, as well.

One of them might have gotten up to make a trip the bathroom. Both of them wouldn't have.

She pushed upright and looked around the darkened room. The security lights, as few and far between as they were, were still enough to bathe the room in a pale glow that showed her with one sweeping glance that she was alone. The lingering dregs of sleep abandoned her abruptly.

A shiver went through her as she listened intently to the night sounds of the city. The siren grew louder for a few moments and then stopped. Kate's heart clenched painfully when it did.

Scrambling from the bed, she moved to the window and peered out. The cabin they'd been given was a good distance back from the street, but she was sure she would've still been able to see flashing lights if the police car was anywhere nearby.

The room wasn't particularly cold, but she still felt a chill creep over her as she stood uneasily by the window, peering through the darkness in hope of seeing some sign of Sergei or Silvair. Finally, she moved away from the window and began to pull her jeans on, which she'd discarded when she'd gone to bed.

Moving to the window Sergei had left propped open, she pushed it up high enough to remove the drawer he'd wedged under it and closed and locked the window. The door, she discovered, was still locked and bolted.

They'd gone out the window.

Trying not to think why they might have done that, she dragged one of the chairs over to the door and wedged it under the doorknob and then dragged the other to use it to barricade the bathroom door.

The urge to pee assailed her as soon as she'd blocked the access to the bathroom. After a brief debate, she listened intently at the door and finally moved the chair and went in to use the toilet, dashing back to the main room as soon as she'd finished and shoving the chair under the knob again.

Too tired to pace and too anxious to sleep, she finally compromised by moving to the bed and perching against the headboard with her knees drawn up to her chest.

Where would they go? And why?

Why would they go out the window instead of the door?

She knew why. She just didn't want to accept it.

She'd struggled for days to dismiss what she'd seen, what she knew was real and not merely a figment of a shocked mind. Whatever Sergei and Silvair were, they weren't – human. She hadn't just seen them take the forms of the Siberian tiger and the African lion. It wasn't just all the little things she'd noted that added up to support her 'wild imagination'. Neither the lion nor the tiger had ever behaved the way she knew they should have behaved if they were nothing more than wild beasts.

As drugged up as they'd been, neither one had ever made any attempt to harm her—far from it. They'd tried to protect her from Panas when he'd started slapping her around.

It was no comfort to accept all that.

She still didn't understand why they'd changed *tonight* and gone out.

They *must* be able to control the change.

Getting up at that thought, she moved to the window to peer out again, this time at the sky. A crescent moon floated near the cityscape horizon.

"They aren't werewolves," she muttered irritably to herself. Still, if they were were-felines, wouldn't the same rules apply?

Except she didn't think they were were-felines. She wasn't certain why, but she had the feeling the feline form was their 'natural' form. They'd never seemed particularly comfortable in human form, she decided, but did that mean she was right? And even if she was, there should be some 'rules' to it, shouldn't there?

Maybe, but if there were, it didn't necessarily follow that Hollywood had it right. In fact, it seemed unlikely. The stories the writers created were from old myths and legends, retold so many times now there might not be so much as a grain of the real truth to them.

Except the part where they changed from human to beast and back again—at will, or by some internal clock, or external stimulus.

She didn't know, but the longer she sat waiting for them to return, listening absently to distant sirens, the more uneasy she was.

She couldn't shake the feeling that the activity was related to the absence of Silvair and Sergei.

"It's probably just a fire," she told herself, mentally trying to count the number of sirens she'd heard since she'd first awakened. She hadn't heard any fire engine horns, though. A wreck? That couldn't be it. There would still have been a fire truck on the scene.

She was still trying to convince herself that she was wrong when she heard a heavy thud from the bathroom that made her heart clench to a painful halt in her chest. Paralyzed, she listened for another sound and nearly jumped out of her skin when something heavy hit the bathroom door. The door knob jiggled.

A squeak of terror erupted from her throat before she could stop it as something slammed against the doorknob and it abruptly fell off. Bounding off the bed, she stared in absolute horror at the door as someone, or something, shoved against it.

Abruptly, the sounds came together in her mind. "Sergei?" she asked shakily. "Silvair?"

A deep rumbling sound answered. Feeling faint with relief, she charged toward the door on unsteady legs and dragged the chair away before he could slam against it again and break it from its hinges. The tiger stood on the other side of the door, his legs braced. His hind legs wobbled and gave out abruptly.

"Oh god! Sergei?"

Flipping the light on, Kate blinked to adjust her vision in the sudden brightness and then stared in dismay at the blood oozing from his hip. A brightly tufted dart of some kind was embedded in his side.

Surging toward him abruptly, she grabbed the end of the dart and pulled it out, staring at it blankly for several moments before it dawned on her that it must be a tranquilizer dart. The tiger dropped heavily to his side, his breathing labored.

As horrified as she was, the sound of sirens pierced her shock.

"They're coming here! They're looking for you!"

Whirling her head, she stared toward the window, hoping she was wrong. The flash of neon blue and red lights banished the forlorn hope. Pushing to her feet, she looked around the room frantically for some place to hide him. It was a short search. The room wasn't big and it was virtually empty—certainly didn't contain anything big enough to hide a huge Siberian tiger.

The bathtub?

"No! They'll look there for sure."

Under the bed?

She turned to survey the bed doubtfully and finally rushed over and dropped to her knees. The bed was not only low to the floor, it was sitting on some kind of platform, not a bed frame. Sergei was in no condition to run any further, though, and she doubted he could even get out the window again.

She rushed back to him, grabbing his head and lifting it. "Change, Sergei! They're looking for a tiger. Change back!"

He stared at her, his gaze vacant and unfocused, and a sense of doom spread through her. She could hear the slamming of doors—car doors. The cops had seen him come this way. In a few minutes, the sound of voices joined the tramp of feet. The beams of flashlights crossed the front window.

Dashing to the bed, Kate grabbed the mattress and heaved it off. Grasping the box springs beneath, she heaved it up and shoved it back against the mattress and then dashed back to the bathroom. "Sergei!" she said in a harsh whisper. "Get up, baby. Come on."

He opened his eyes and stared at her as she tugged at him.

She discovered there were tears streaming down her cheeks as she tugged and pulled at him, trying to get him on his feet. She couldn't budge him. Grasping his head, she hefted it upward until he was looking at her. "Get up, damn it! I can't carry you!"

His gaze seemed to focus for a moment. He lifted his head from her grip and heaved himself unsteadily to his feet. Swiping at the tears with one hand, she put her arm around him and guided him toward the bed frame, staggering under his weight as he struggled to keep his balance. Stepping over the low frame with an obvious effort, he dropped to the floor and rolled onto his side.

Kate stared at him, trying to still the wobble in her chin. "Just be quiet, baby. Ok? I'll do something for that wound as soon as they're gone."

He lifted his head to watch her when she grabbed the box springs and carefully lowered them over the frame again. Praying she wasn't going to suffocate him, she repositioned the mattress and grabbed the sheets to straighten them.

Light flashed in the front window while she was trying to remake the bed and her heart fluttered painfully in her chest as she whirled to look and saw the outline of a man on the other side.

Someone started hammering at her door. Covering her mouth to stifle a gasp, she stared at the door, trying to force her mind to supply her with a 'normal' reaction to a pounding on her door in the middle of the night. "Who is it?" she finally called out in a quavering voice.

"Police, ma'am. Can you open the door?"

"I-I was asleep. What is it?"

"Could you just open the door, ma'am? I'd like to speak with you."

"Uh … yes … just a minute."

She glanced around the room a little frantically, wondering what evidence might be visible if they decided to push their way into the room to check it.

Sergei had been bleeding! Scrambling on tiptoes toward the bathroom, she grabbed the damp towels and mopped the blood off the bathroom floor and then followed the trail of drops to the bed, scrubbing at the carpet.

The hammering started again while she was trying to decide where to hide the towels. Shoving them under the pile of linens she'd left on the floor, she moved to the door and opened it a crack, leaving the security chain on.

She stared at the uniformed officer on the other side of the door. "What is it?" she gasped breathlessly.

"A tiger escaped from the zoo, ma'am."

"A tiger?" she echoed, gasping it out in shocked disbelief without any effort since she was horrified to have her worst fears realized.

"And a lion. We've captured the lion, but the tiger's still on the loose, and wounded. He'll be dangerous until the tranq takes him down."

Kate gaped at him. She licked her lips. "You killed the lion?" she asked faintly.

"Captured him."

"B-but not the tiger?"

"I just wanted to make you aware of the danger. You should stay in your room until we find the tiger."

Kate nodded jerkily, wondering a little sickly what they'd done with poor Silvair. She'd almost managed to close the door again when another cop rounded the cabin.

"The bathroom window's out."

The cop at the door slammed his palm against it before she could slam and lock it. "We need to come in for a look."

"Why?"

"The bathroom window's been busted out."

Kate stared at him blankly, trying to think up a lie. "Oh—that. I was trying to get the window open and it just fell out."

"We'd like to come in for a look."

"B—but—I'm not dressed!" Kate said a little desperately. "The tiger isn't in here!"

"Open the door ma'am!"

Kate glared at him. "Well give me a minute to put some clothes on!"

She felt faint with relief when he allowed her to close the door. Flipping the overhead light on, she checked her clean up job and then dropped to the side of the bed. "They're coming in. Just be quiet," she whispered, hoping he understood her.

When she'd opened the door, she moved to the bed and sat down gingerly on the edge, crossing her arms over her chest and watching the two cops as they prowled the room and then went into the bathroom to examine it.

"You here alone?"

Kate frowned at him. "Did you see anybody else?" she snapped.

One of the cops picked up a pair of men's jeans.

She stared at the jeans in dismay. "My boyfriend. Those belong to my boyfriend."

He picked up another pair of jeans and looked at her.

"Is there a *law* against having two pairs of jeans?"

The cops eyed her suspiciously. "You turning tricks?"

Kate gaped at him. "I told you he's my boyfriend!"

"He left without his pants?" the other cop asked sarcastically.

Kate glared at him. "He has *three* pairs of jeans! He was wearing the other pair when he left."

"What's your boyfriend's name?"

"Sergei."

"Sergei what?"

Kate blinked at him, struggling to shake a name loose from her blank mind. "Siber—uh—rof." She smiled weakly. "He's Russian. I have the worst time with his name."

"Where did he go?"

"Who?"

The two cops exchanged a look. "Your boyfriend."

"He was hungry. He went out to see if he could find a place to get something to eat."

"And left you here by yourself?"

"I was sleepy, so I went to bed, and then you started banging on my door and woke me up. You said you were looking for a tiger. Do you see a tiger? Because I don't see a tiger, and that being the case, I'd like to know what the hell you're doing in my damned room when you're supposed to be looking for an escaped tiger!"

The two cops exchanged another look. After looking around the room again, however, they finally departed.

Slumping with relief, Kate locked the door again and shoved the chair back under the knob. She felt like yielding to a fit of hysterics, but she couldn't afford the luxury. Afraid to completely turn the bed over again when the cops were still prowling the area, she simply shoved at the mattress and box springs until she could peer down at Sergei.

He was so still it frightened her until she noticed he was breathing slowly and evenly. The tranq had undoubtedly knocked him out. Deciding she wouldn't find a better time to examine his wound, she moved down to look at it. To her relief, the bleeding had stopped. The blood that had run down his leg was drying.

She found the bullet on the floor beside his hip. Frowning, she picked it up and studied it doubtfully, but it was definitely a bullet.

He'd been shot before—when he'd stolen the picnic basket. The next time she'd noticed the wound it was closed and healing. Dare she hope this would be the same? Or was this wound worse? He'd said that bullet had passed through, but he wouldn't let her look at it. Maybe his body had pushed it out as it seemed to have pushed the slug from this wound?

It had to have been the bullet they'd shot him with. Regardless of the no doubt ill repute of the establishment they were in, it just didn't seem likely there'd already been a bullet just lying on the floor under the bed.

She sat back on her heels when she realized she couldn't do anything *but* hope. She couldn't get a doctor for him—or a vet. In either form trying to bring someone to see about him would be the same as turning him over to the authorities.

They had Silvair. She felt sick to her stomach at the thought, but what, if anything, could she do about it?

Sitting upright again, she leaned down to stroke Sergei's

side. The warmth of his body reassured her. After a few moments, she rose and pushed the mattress and box springs back until only a small wedge of space remained. She doubted the frame was air tight, but she didn't see any sense in taking a chance he might not be able to get enough air.

Moving to the light switch, she turned off the overhead light and then the one in the bathroom. When she returned to the main room, she carefully pulled the window curtain aside enough to peer out. She could still see cops wandering around some of the cabins, but contrary to the orders issued to her to stay put and the lateness, there were knots of people here and there, watching the proceedings.

The fear of being caught receded a little, allowing her focus to shift to Silvair. She didn't know if she could help him, but she wasn't going to find out hiding in the room.

What if the cops came back, though?

She shook that thought off. There was no reason why they should.

Sneak out the back? Or walk brazenly out the front door?

She didn't like the idea of leaving the door open like an invitation for the cops to come back to snoop. Besides, she had the feeling if they saw her they'd decide she was trying to sneak off and that would translate in a cop mind to guilt.

Slipping her shoes on, she headed into the bathroom and peered out the window. When she didn't see any sign of the cops, she dragged the chair she'd been using for a barricade inside, climbed onto the seat and, after peering around one last time, stepped onto the edge and leapt over the window and glass lying beneath it.

She was weak and shaky just from sneaking through the dark by the time she'd cleared the motel area and reached the street. Walking as casually as she could, she crossed the street, heading toward the activity she could see down the block. There was a fair sized crowd of gawkers, she discovered, more people than she'd seen around the motel—more cops, too. She counted at least four marked cars and one unmarked car with a light on the roof. They'd cordoned off a section of the street and cop stood at the corner to redirect the little bit of traffic flowing through the intersection at the corner. About half way down the block, she saw a large panel truck. Even as she peered toward it an angry roar issued from one of the cages she could see in the back.

Her heart stilled and then began to hammer double time.

Dismay filled her.

There were people everywhere.

She made her way down the street anyway with the half formed thought of trying to discover where the truck would be taking Silvair. There was a zoo logo on the side.

They had to know it wasn't *their* lion and tiger, Kate thought in dismay. Maybe they already knew, or suspected, that the felines they'd spotted were the same ones being hunted in her area. Did that mean they'd be taking him to the zoo anyway? Or taking him to destroy him?

If they knew about the killings in the club, or discovered it, they'd kill him. So maybe they hadn't known at first or they wouldn't have brought Silvair down with a tranq dart and tried to take Sergei down with one. Or maybe they just hadn't wanted a bunch of cowboy cops shooting up the town and maybe killing bystanders in the process?

It didn't matter. He was dead if they got him where they could kill him without having to worry about killing any bystanders.

A sense of desolation washed over her. She struggled against it, trying to think if there was anything she could do, trying *not* to consider why she felt the desolation or the desperation to do something to help him. It flickered through her mind to wonder *why* she'd taken such a chance to protect Sergei—why she was standing in the middle of the street contemplating some way to free Silvair. She'd just spent a week and half trying to figure out how to get away from them. *This* was her chance.

The thought made her ill instead of giving her any sense of relief as it should have.

Thrusting it aside, she began to work her way toward the truck until she could see Silvair pacing one of the two cages in the back—three steps one way, three steps back. It wasn't any bigger than the cage Panas had had him in. He roared again when he reached the door of the cage, his glowing eyes full of hate as he stared out at the crowd. A knot of misery welled in her chest. Even as she stared at him, fighting the sting of tears in her nose and eyes, he turned his head and looked directly at her for a long moment. His brows twitched together and then he looked away. Turning, he moved to the back of the cage and settled heavily in the shadows.

He didn't look in her direction again.

Swallowing against the painful knot in her throat, she began to inch a little closer, pausing every few minutes to glance around as casually as she could. Nobody seemed to be paying her much attention. They were staring at the lion in the cage, or watching the cops.

When she'd moved as close as she could, she examined the cage. It was secured with a bolt lock. She could open it if she could just get to it, but what then? They'd shoot him down for sure if she released him in this crowd. He might get away in the pandemonium that was sure to follow, and he might not.

The back of the truck had a roll down door but it looked like the cage was too close to the back edge to actually close it. Undoubtedly, they'd had to move it by hand and hadn't been able to push it further back after they'd gotten Silvair in it. There was no sign of a fork lift.

It was dark inside. She couldn't see if the truck contained anything else, but the shadows themselves would be deep enough to conceal her if she could just find a way to get in. She shifted uneasily, looking around at the crowd again.

Most of the people, she saw, had stopped staring at the lion once he moved to the shadows, but there was a cop stationed at the rear of the truck. A helicopter passed overhead, low enough it seemed to attract the attention of most of the people in the street. Seizing the moment, Kate walked briskly to the truck, stepped on the bumper and climbed inside, fully expecting any moment that someone would grab her and haul her out again. She felt almost faint when no one did. Scurrying toward the cab end, she crouched in the shadows, struggling with the shaky weakness that washed over her. The lion, she discovered when she finally managed to catch her breath, was staring at her. She could see the gleam of his eyes.

It was Silvair. She knew it had to be. She was still uneasy, and still afraid to even try to talk to him. What good would it do anyway? It wasn't as if he could talk back.

The anxiety that Sergei would be found while she was trapped in the truck and unable to leave again blossomed inside of her and began to grow. She must have spent a terror filled hour crouched behind the cage, waiting, expecting to be discovered, afraid they'd catch Sergei and find her when they put him in the other cage. Finally, she heard the door of the cab open and slam closed again. The back began to vibrate as the engine roared to life. The faint jolt as the truck began to pull away rocked her.

Chapter Thirteen

Kate's heart leapt into her throat and tried to choke her as adrenaline shot into her blood stream. She hadn't really formulated a plan. She'd been too terrified she was going to get caught, too certain of it to consider what she was going to do after she got inside the truck. As soon as the truck had put some distance between her and the crowded streets, though, she began to make her way around the cage, wondering if they were going to have to jump out of the moving truck.

They would if the truck made it to the freeway before she managed to get the cage open.

She missed the first traffic light stop. Making her way carefully to the front of the cage, she clung to the bars with one hand and worked at the bolt with the other, trying to ignore the rush of pavement in her peripheral vision as the truck picked up speed. Fortunately, either because they'd had to leave the back open or because the truck was heavy enough it took a while to build up speed, they weren't traveling very fast.

It still seemed fast when she was hanging out of the back of a truck.

The bolt was stiff. She was sweating—either from exertion or fear or both by the time she managed to work it loose. She didn't realize until she had that she was clinging to the cage door itself. She realized it then because it swung outward, taking her with it. She sucked in a horrified gasp as she swung out over the street, clinging frantically to the bar.

She was trying to decide whether to try to leap off or cling to the bars until the truck slowed, wondering if she even had the option, when she felt the truck begin to decelerate. The cage door swung inward with the movement. She sucked in another breath of fright as she swung toward the cage again, expecting the door to bang loud enough to alert the driver.

Silvair caught the swinging door with his body. She winced

as it slammed into him. The momentum as the truck braked to a stop made him stagger back. Kate pried her fingers from the bars and dropped toward the pavement. It was further than she'd expected. Her knees buckled when she made contact and she sprawled in the road. Silvair hit the pavement almost on top of her.

A car horn blared. Scrambling to her feet, Kate launched herself into a run as the lion bounded away. The bastard driving the car laid down on his horn, frantically trying to alert the truck driver.

Kate didn't dare look back. She ran after Silvair as fast as she could. Behind her, she heard the squeal of brakes and knew the truck had stopped. Someone yelled at her to stop. She ran faster, rounding a building and ducking into the alley she'd seen Silvair race in to. Blinded the moment she left the lighted mouth of the alley, she plowed into a solid form. Hands grabbed her. She sucked in a breath to scream.

"Shhh!" Silvair growled. "It is I, sveety."

Grabbing her hand as the weakness of relief went through her, he tugged her into a run and led her through the alley. He pulled her to a stop at the other end. "I have a problem, I tink," he muttered.

"What?" Kate gasped breathlessly.

"No clothes. You tink people notice more de lion? Or de naked man?"

There was a trace of humor in his voice. "Shit! I didn't think about that!"

He dragged her up and kissed her briefly on the mouth. "Bad Katie! Ve have to do vat ve can."

A touch of irritation flickered through her that he sounded so nonchalant about the situation.

Actually, he sounded almost exhilarated.

"Ve should move fast. De cops will swarm here soon."

They kept to the alleys as much as possible, hiding in the shadows as the police cars zipped up and down the streets, making their way unerringly toward the motel again. "Sergei, he get away. Silvair not so lucky," he muttered.

"Not clean away. He was shot," Kate said shakily.

Silvair shot her a sharp look, but the shadows were too deep for her to tell anything about his expression.

"I sneaked out the bathroom window," she told him once the motel was in sight.

He nodded, glancing up and down the street. There were still loiterers. "I'm tinking dey notice if I stroll across de street naked. You go. I circle 'round and meet you dere."

She didn't want to leave him even though she could see the sense of what he'd said. "You'll be careful?"

"I doan like de cage. Doan like de holes dey put in my hide more." Placing a hand in the middle of her back, he nudged her with one hand to encourage her to go.

Sucking in a sustaining breath, Kate glanced at the street again and then stepped out of the alley and walked briskly toward the motel. Several of the people on the street, mostly men, turned to stare at her speculatively, but, thankfully, none of them approached her. It still sent a quiver of uneasiness through her. She had a bad feeling the driver of the car and the truck driver had gotten a pretty good look at her. If nothing else, they were bound to have noticed her long red hair.

She made it to the back of the cabin without incident, but she was still trying to climb in when Silvair joined her. Grasping her waist, he lifted her up so that she could climb through the opening. He grinned at her when he saw the chair on the other side.

Sergei, as naked as Silvair, met them at the door to the bathroom as they emerged. After staring at them a moment, he moved across the room unsteadily and retrieved his jeans. Silvair followed suit. "I doan tink we should stay here. Katie, she bust me out. De cops runnin' around like a swarm of bees."

Sergei slid a speculative glance at Kate and nodded. "We go out de back."

Exhausted as she was from only a few hours sleep, Kate was still buzzing from spurts of adrenaline. She didn't argue. The cops weren't likely to give up hunting. They'd just call in more and more people to help with the search.

They'd walked several blocks when Silvair began to study

the vehicles along the curb. Finally choosing an old, dark sedan, he glanced around casually, and then busted the glass from the driver's window with his fist. Sliding under the wheel, he reached to unlock the other doors and then dove under the dash. A few moments later, the engine roared to life.

Kate, who'd reluctantly climbed into the back seat, watched him in open mouthed surprise. A car thief couldn't have boosted the car any quicker or more efficiently.

She didn't say anything. What would be the point? Getting caught for stealing the car was probably the least of their worries. She sat tensely in the back until Silvair pulled the car onto the freeway. By the time they reached the outskirts of the city, her weariness caught up with her and she dozed off.

The deceleration in their speed roused her some time later and she lifted her head and stared at the city they were entering. The neon signs everywhere she looked were enough to identify the city. Leaving the freeway, Silvair cruised the streets of Las Vegas until they reached the seedy side of town and then left even that behind for an industrial district. Finally, near dawn, he parked the car outside of a junkyard and they all got out and began walking in the pre-dawn morning.

They walked for what seemed like miles before Silvair stopped to survey a derelict building. Making their way around it until they found a way in, they went inside, explored the building until they found a place to settle in reasonable comfort and sat down to rest.

Kate was still exhausted, mostly emotionally wrung out, she thought. She looked at Sergei and then Silvair a little doubtfully. "You aren't going to leave me again if I go to sleep?"

The two exchanged an uncomfortable look. "We be here when you wake up, Katie," Sergei said finally, tugging her toward him and shifting her around until her cheek rested against his chest. It wasn't particularly comfortable, but she fell asleep anyway. The building was bright when she woke again, and both her stomach and Sergei's was rumbling with hunger.

Yawning, she pushed away from him and sat up, stretching. She discovered new muscles she'd overexerted in the disaster the night before and winced. Sighing, she rubbed the sleep from her face. "What's the plan now?" she asked tiredly.

Both Sergei and Silvair were studying her when she looked up, frowning thoughtfully. "We buy a car," Silvair responded finally. "I'm tinking we should get far away from the udder place."

Relief filled her. "Good idea. I don't think stealing another one would be the way to go." She frowned thoughtfully. "We should probably get a newspaper and try to get a car from a private owner. None of us have identification and we'd need that if we went to a car lot. We still need to get some clothes. I don't suppose you've got enough to get me a few things?" she asked, hopeful and embarrassed to have to ask at the same time. "I've got a little money in the bank, but I couldn't get it out without identification."

They delved into their pockets and dragged out the rolls of cash each of them were carrying. Kate counted it, chewing her lower lip when she'd finished as she calculated how much it was likely to take to buy what they needed and still get to the coast. "I don't think there's going to be enough to pay for passage on a ship by the time we get to the coast, even if we get a really cheap car—and we want to make sure we get something that'll make it to the coast.

"You two should stay here while I go take care of the shopping."

She could tell they didn't like that idea when they ignored the suggestion and got up to leave.

"You're going to attract a lot of attention."

Sergei shrugged. "Dey are looking for de felines."

"You've got a point," Kate admitted, capitulating, mostly because she didn't really relish walking through the bad part of town by herself. She'd been lucky she managed what she had the night before without getting mugged or raped. If she'd had time to think about it, then, she would've been scared half to death.

She also didn't particularly care for the idea of walking all the way into town and back again lugging what she'd bought.

They stopped at the first greasy fast food place they came to and bought food and drinks. Neither Sergei nor Silvair seemed favorably impressed with the food. She wasn't for that matter, but none of them were dressed for anything else and, besides, she knew they would have to handle the money carefully to pay for everything. They paused at a phone booth to find the address of a second hand shop. Emerging from the store a few hours later with a couple of changes of clothing for each of them and two pairs of the biggest shoes she could find, they ducked into the first alley they came to and changed clothes.

She could see from the pained looks on both men's faces that the shoes didn't fit that well, but when she suggested stopping to find something that fit better, they declined.

"We need to stop somewhere anyway," she said reasonably. "I've got to get something to color my hair before I'm recognized. I should probably cut it, too," she added reluctantly.

"No!" both of the men said at once.

She glanced at them in irritated surprise, tempted to inform them that it was her hair and she'd do what she damned well pleased with it, but the truth was she didn't especially want to cut it. She didn't mind coloring it. She'd never liked the brassy red Panas had insisted on.

Finding a low priced department store, she left them outside and went in to collect a few toiletries. Neither of them had shaved, naturally enough, in more than a week and they'd begun to look pretty scruffy even though their facial hair didn't seem to grow very fast. After a brief debate over disguise versus clean shaven, she bought razors and shaving cream. She didn't know if they'd been seen clean shaven or not, but the beards made them look *more* dangerous and she thought it was a good idea to make them 'blend' as much as possible.

Finding that he didn't especially like being surrounded by so many man-children, Sergei surveyed the building and the field of cars around it and finally sauntered around to the shady side of the building to wait. Silvair trailed along behind him, settling with his back against the wall of the building when Sergei stopped.

"How bad you tink we fuck up last night?" Sergei asked

after a few moments.

Silvair considered it. "Vid Katie?"

Sergei frowned. "You tink we fuck up wid Katie?"

"Ah! You mean de police mans, eh?"

Sergei discovered he'd lost interest in the previous subject. "You tink we fuck up wid Katie?"

Silvair shrugged. "She know vat we are now."

"She know dat after we kill de beeg cat," Sergei pointed out.

"She act strange after dat," Silvair agreed. "I'm tinking she doan believe what she see den."

Sergei had thought that, too. She hadn't been surprised or frightened—of him, anyway—when he'd come through the bathroom window the night before, though. His memory was a little faulty. Between the gunshot wound and the tranq, he'd been pretty woozy, but he clearly remembered the look on her face when she'd seen him. She'd approached him without any hesitancy. Worry and fear had been etched on her face, but not *of* him—*for* him. She'd hidden him, lied to protect him—like a mate.

He'd thought so, anyway, until he discovered she'd gone after Silvair to free him.

Not that he wouldn't have if he'd been in any condition to help him, but that was because he'd begun to think of Silvair as friend, even though he wasn't tiger, despite their rivalry for Kate.

"She was not surprised when she saw me again last night, or afraid," he said finally. "She hide me from de police mans. She lied to de police mans to protect me. Den she leave and go to you. I doan tink I understand dat."

Silvair stared at him, not particularly pleased to hear it, though he'd suspected something of the sort, known she hadn't given either of them away when she'd had the chance. He'd been ashamed when she'd seen him caged, embarrassed that she'd had to come to help him, but he'd been pleased that she'd been willing to risk capture herself to help him. He'd thought, hoped, that meant she'd begun to think of him as a mate. "I doan tink I understand, neither," he said irritably.

"Dis is like she would do for friend, da?" Sergei asked, but he didn't really need clarification since he knew that was what he would've done for Silvair.

"Is goot she tink of us as friends," Silvair said morosely.

"You tink? I doan tink so. I doan wanna be Katie's friend."

Silvair glared at him. "You tol' me you was not tinking of Katie as a mate."

"I said I didn't tink it would work. I didn't say I didn't want it."

"Sound to me like dat's what you was saying!" Silvair said indignantly.

They glowered at one another challengingly for several moments. Finally, with the reflection that this was a very bad place to try to settle their dispute with any sort of battle, Sergei forced some of the tension from his body and shrugged. "Doan matter no ways—what you tink, what I tink. She din pick neidder one of us. She still talkin' 'bout takin' us to de ship."

"'Cause we doan tol' her we been tinking 'bout stayin' here."

Sergei frowned. "You tink if we say dat den she might consider picking one of us?"

Silvair thought he didn't want the competition. "She still a man-child. Dey say doan work to mate wid no man-child."

"Maybe I doan care if I doan get no cub!"

"Maybe I doan care neidder!" Silvair growled.

Stalemate, Sergei thought angrily, and they still didn't know whether she would even find the idea acceptable. It didn't follow that she would just because she seemed to have accepted what they were. Try as he might, he couldn't think of anything she'd done or said that seemed to indicate she favored him over Silvair, or vice versa, which was comforting but not an answer. Not the one he wanted anyway. He frowned. "I'm tinking it might not be a good ting to stay here no ways," he said grumpily. "These man-childs, dey doan never sleep. Why dey out roamin' 'round in de middle of de night, anyways? How we gonna get food if dey doan sleep no time?"

Silvair shrugged. He'd thought it was safe enough to go out for a hunt himself, and he was used to living near the man-cities. On the other hand, after over a week of only being able to snatch a quick meal here and there to keep Kate from discovering them, they'd both been too hungry to use the caution they should have. It hadn't helped that they'd been in a hurry to get back to Kate before she discovered they were missing. "Not gonna be able to roam here," he agreed. "Not anywhere near their cities no ways."

Despite his irritation a faint smile curled Sergei's lips after a moment when he remembered the way she'd coaxed and bullied him until he'd gotten up to hide in the place she'd found for him. He'd been too tired and in too much pain to care if they found him or not. He hadn't felt like moving and he'd been irritated with her for her persistence. He only dimly recalled the conversation she'd had with the police, he'd been too near unconsciousness, but he thought she'd done well considering how frightened she was.

"What you smilin' 'bout?" Silvair asked irritably.

"I was tinkin' 'bout de way Katie handle dem police mans last night." A memory surfaced that he'd forgotten, though how he could've when it had pleased him so much he didn't know. "She tol' dem I was her man." She hadn't used those words—he couldn't remember her exact words—but he could tell from the other things that had been said that that was what she'd meant.

Silvair slid a narrow eyed glare at him. "She lef you though and come get me out of dat cage."

Sergei scowled at him. "She wouldn't have had to if you'd done like I tol' you!" he growled.

"I didn't catch no bullet," Silvair retorted.

"'Cause dey didn't need no bullet. You done keel ober wid de drugs."

"'Cause I was tryin' to divert dem from you wid your pale pelt! Dat flashy pelt no goot for dis place!"

"If you blend in dey wouldn't have shot you wid dat dart!"

Silvair was about to defend both his actions and his beautiful pelt when he spotted Kate looking for them. Surging to his feet, he glanced at Sergei and flung a parting shot at him before stalking off to join Kate. "My pelt blend better dan yours, and it's more pretty, too!"

* * * *

Deciding they looked a little more respectable, Kate looked for a little higher class hotel. It didn't look a lot better than the one they'd stayed in, briefly, the night before, but it was a definite improvement—still old and worn, but cleaner by far. Sergei and Silvair both dragged their shoes off and threw them down as soon as they were inside. Smiling, she pulled the new shoes she'd bought them out of her shopping bag and then left them scanning the newspapers and commandeered the bathroom to color her hair.

She doubted it would be a fruitful search, for all that. They could barely *speak* English. It seemed unlikely they could read it. Silvair proved her wrong. By the time she'd finished with her hair, he'd not only circled a dozen possibilities but had begun calling the phone numbers to check on them.

Sergei did a double take when she came out of the bathroom as a brunette. It was hard to tell from his expression whether he approved the change or not. "This is the closest I could find to my natural hair color," she said a little defensively. "It isn't really red. Panas made me bleach it."

"I like dat," Sergei said finally. "Maybe I should color my hair?"

Kate gaped at him in dismay. "But—it's beautiful! You don't really want to make it brown—do you?"

He sent Silvair a smug look she found confusing.

Silvair, already annoyed with the difficulty he was having making himself understood, glared at his back as he headed into the bathroom for a shower. "You doan like dat wash out color of his?" he demanded.

"It's not …." She stopped, realizing abruptly that Silvair was jealous of her comment about Sergei's hair. "Yes, I do," she said, firmly repressing the urge to smile at their vanity. "I like yours, too."

Obviously pleased, he glanced toward the bathroom to see if Sergei had heard. He frowned when he heard the shower.

"Why don't I make the phone calls?" Kate said, as much to distract him from the brooding quarrel with Sergei as because she'd seen how frustrated he was that he was having such a hard time making himself understood. "You can tell me what you want me to ask them."

Shrugging, he handed her the newspaper and they worked their way through several more of the listings while Sergei bathed. He emerged some fifteen minutes later, stark naked and with water still glistening on his skin and dripping from his hair. The sight was enough to completely distract Kate.

Sergei, apparently oblivious, sprawled on the bed, grabbed the remote and began to flip through the TV channels.

Silvair's eyes were narrowed on her when Kate finally managed to gather her wits and focus on the phone, but it was the voice on the other end of the line that had actually broken the spell—sort of. She felt uncomfortably warm and more than a little breathless.

Leaving her to finish the phone call on her own, Silvair headed to bathroom to bathe and shave, she supposed, as Sergei had.

She didn't manage to get much information regarding the car she'd called about, but then it was far too expensive to her mind anyway. Thanking the man for his time, she hung up and tried to focus on reading the listings. Most of the cars Silvair had circled, she discovered, were well above their means. Deciding he probably didn't know the currency even if he could read English, she struggled for a little while to find affordable alternatives but the plain fact was she couldn't get her mind off of Sergei.

It wasn't that she hadn't noticed how gorgeous he was, how wonderfully well built—she had—and she'd thought he was sexy even scruffy with a week and half's growth of beard. Somehow her memory of just how handsome he was clean shaven had dimmed, though.

The urge to crawl over him and lick the moisture from his body swept over her from seemingly nowhere, bringing with it a wall of heat.

Chapter Fourteen

Struggling to tamp the wayward thoughts, refusing to yield to the urge to simply drop the newspaper and stare at him, Kate focused determinedly on the classified ads, but she discovered she couldn't seem to absorb anything she read.

She'd never approached him for sex. She hadn't felt a need to. He had a healthy appetite and he hadn't left her wanting.

She'd more sex in the ten days she'd been with Sergei and Silvair than she'd had the ten months before than. She shouldn't feel so—hungry.

He'd think she'd lost her mind.

Or worse, he'd think she was only doing it because she wanted something.

Which she did—him.

She wasn't certain she had the nerve to be the aggressor. It wasn't that she never *had*. She'd initiated sex with her former boyfriend once or twice—mostly to please him, not because she'd felt the need or any real desire to do so. She was passive by nature.

But why shouldn't she, she thought? What could he say, no?

And then she'd be embarrassed, but she didn't think he would say no.

Feeling shaky, she set the paper aside, got up and moved across the room to stand at the foot of the bed. Sergei's gaze moved from the TV to her the moment she rose, increasing both her nervousness and her heat index. Her hands were shaking slightly as she dropped the towel she'd been wearing.

Sergei followed the movement. She noticed the tension in him when he met her gaze again, but he didn't move. Peeling her panties off, she dropped them to the floor, as well, and placed first one knee and then the other onto the end of the bed. Crawling toward him, she paused to skate a hand along one of his splayed legs. The muscles rippled beneath her palm, but otherwise he remained still, watchful.

Dipping as she reached his thighs, she lathed her tongue along the hair roughed skin and then nipped at it lightly.

She'd more than half expected him to seize the initiative when she approached him. He didn't. He remained as perfectly still as a statue. She was disconcerted briefly, but the taut set of his features and the tumult in his eyes told her he wasn't indifferent, wasn't uninterested. He was controlling himself because he wanted to see what she would do.

Emboldened by that certainty, she moved closer, licking the moisture from his belly and chest as she'd imagined doing. The rippling of his flesh beneath her mouth as she followed with light brushes of her lips and gentle, nipping bites assured her she hadn't misinterpreted his stillness.

Indecision hit her as she made her way down his taut belly again. Up? Or down? An image of kissing her way upward to his hard mouth and then climbing astride his lap and mounting his turgid shaft teased her mind, tempting her. It was supplanted by an image of her pleasuring him with her mouth and, abruptly, she knew that was what she wanted. After all the times he'd taken her to the heights of mindless pleasure, she wanted to do that to him, wanted to know if she could.

She made her way downward after a moment's hesitation, teasing him by placing nibbling kisses all the way around his cock, ignoring it at is it nudged against her cheek and her neck in passing. She hesitated again when she reached the juncture of his cock and his balls, not from any doubt, but to tease him. He sucked in a harsh breath when she flattened her tongue against the underside of his shaft and dragged it slowly upward. Taking only the head into her mouth when she reached the tip, she sucked it, teasing the sensitive rim with her tongue, tracing the slit in the tip and then sucking at him again.

He let out a hissing breath, clamping his hands almost painfully on her shoulders.

She paused, lifting her head to look at him.

His eyes were squeezed tightly shut, his face contorted as if he was in agony.

Her belly clenched, moisture squeezing from the walls of her sex to flood her channel with heated need. Sucking in a shaky breath, she returned her attention to cock, alternately stroking it with one hand and enveloping it in the heat of her mouth to suck on his flesh. His hands kneaded her shoulders and then moved to settle on her head, guiding her.

She hadn't considered that she might get just as much pleasure from giving it to him, but as his breath grew rougher, as she felt him moving closer and closer to climax, she felt her own body moving closer, felt her hunger growing.

She was so intent on stroking and sucking Sergei's flesh with feverish need that she didn't notice when the bed dipped, didn't realize Silvair had joined them until she felt his hand coast over her buttocks and then delve between to stroke her cleft. She moaned as he slid a thick finger inside of her, pumping it, stroking the walls of her sex.

Shifting her legs wider to give him better access, she curled her hips for him. He moved between her legs, replacing his finger with his cock and another groan escaped her as she felt him pressing into her. She paused, sucking frantically on the piece of flesh in her mouth, holding herself still until he'd pressed fully inside of her and set the pace.

Matching her rhythm to his, she struggled to focus on the twin penetrations, moaning almost incessantly as she felt Sergei building toward release, felt her own body poised on the precipice. Sergei's hands tightened almost crushingly on her head as his cock jerked in her mouth, trying to hold her still. Her heart hammering frantically in her chest, she ignored the warning, pulling at his cock more fiercely with her mouth in her determination to make him cum.

Uttering a deep chested growl, he yielded his seed to her. It seemed to set off a chain reaction. Groaning in ecstasy as her own body convulsed, she swallowed the hot fountain of his bliss, jerking at the force of her release, which seemed to push Silvair over the edge. Catching her hips tightly, he drove deep, grinding against her as came inside of her.

Sucking Sergei's cock one last time as she felt it go flaccid in her mouth, she released it finally, gasping for breath, shivering with the weakness that washed through her. Nuzzling his face against the back of her neck, almost reluctantly, Silvair pulled out of her and settled heavily at the foot of the bed. Before Kate could move, Sergei grasped her beneath the arms and hauled her upward, scooting down the bed as he did so and settling her against his heaving chest.

Dragging in a deep breath, Kate let it out slowly and turned her face to nuzzle it beneath Sergei's chin. Blissfully content, extremely pleased with herself, Kate lay limply against him, drowsing until, eventually, she slipped completely away on the cloud of rapture that engulfed her.

She was alone when she woke and panic instantly washed over her. Sitting up in the bed, she listened intently. Marginally relieved when she didn't hear any sirens, she got up after a few moments and moved to the window to stare out at the street. Without surprise, she saw there was no sign of either of them.

Feeling vaguely abused, still more than a little alarmed, she went into the bathroom to take a quick shower. She saw the note as she was dressing. Surprised, certain at first that it couldn't possibly be a note they'd left her, Kate went to the desk to pick up the folded piece of paper standing there and opened it.

We go for car. Silvair Sergei
"Oh God!"

* * * *

As if Sergei's notable limp since he was shot, and the ugly red wound and accompanying bruises on his beautiful ass weren't enough of a reminder of the disaster liable to follow Sergei and Silvair's ventures in the 'man-child' city, they'd gone off *again*, Kate thought for perhaps the hundredth time as she paced the room, unable to sit still for more than a handful of minutes.

She didn't know why it had taken her so long to see what was as plain to her now as the nose on her face. They weren't *just* foreigners who didn't know their way around the country. They were completely out of their element!

They'd done just fine in the countryside, even though

neither of them were familiar with the area at all, but she didn't think either one of them had ever spent a great deal of time in the world of 'man-children'.

Poor babies!

Poor huge, dangerous, and sometimes really scary babies!

She supposed, considering how easily Silvair had jacked the car they'd drove up in, to say nothing of the fact that he'd done most of the driving, and quite well, he must have spent some time in the cities of his country. She didn't think Sergei had been around man-children much at all, though—and neither one of them really knew how to get along in her world—especially being foreigners on top of everything else!

Dividing her time between staring out the window, flipping through the channels in search of a news channel that might be reporting on their current adventures, and berating herself for sleeping through their departure, Kate was a nervous wreck by the time they returned.

Thankfully, there weren't any sirens to herald their return!

She looked them both over anxiously, but there were no bullet holes in their clothes, no fresh scrapes or scratches to indicate they'd been in a fight or had to flee for their lives. "Did you get a car?" she asked uneasily, more than half expecting to discover they hadn't been able to find any of the addresses and Silvair had decided to jack another car instead of paying for one.

"Ve find nice car," Silvair said agreeably, then shrugged. "De man vant too much."

Relief trickled through her. "I was afraid of that. Most of the cars you circled were practically new. We need to look for something older—something small that's good on gas, preferably.

Sergei shook his head. "Nyet! We like de one we look at, just need more money."

Dismay replaced her momentary relief. "But—you don't even *need* it long. It'd be much better to get something cheap. We'll need money for the trip out to the coast, and then you'll need money to buy passage on a boat. Of course, you could try to sell it when you get there and probably get at least part of the money back, but still …."

The two men exchanged a look she couldn't quite fathom.

Silvair's gaze flickered over her face. "You vant us to leave so much, Katie?" he asked gruffly.

Kate gaped at him. It hadn't occurred to her to consider what she wanted. She hadn't thought in any terms but survival since the night she'd freed them. The moment he asked, though, it hit her like an avalanche that she was never going see either of them again once they got on that ship and sailed away. And that didn't make her feel the way she'd thought she would feel, thought she *should* feel. Moistening her lips, she glanced from Silvair to Sergei.

There'd been a moment in time when that was all she'd wanted or could think about—them leaving so that she'd feel safe, at least from them.

She didn't know when that had changed.

One thing that hadn't changed, though, was that *they* were in danger. "You're not saying you actually want to stay?" she asked instead of answering Silvair's question. "You've been chased, and shot at—*shot*, caged, drugged, beaten—why would you *want* to stay here?"

Both men frowned, exchanged another long look. Sergei shrugged. "It's not so bad here, I'm tinking," he said uncomfortably.

Kate swallowed convulsively. "It's very bad here—for you," she disagreed. "For all of us, really. The cops aren't going to just stop looking. I'll be in trouble myself if they find out I helped you—which I hope they won't, but it's possible. I think the driver of that truck and that asshole in the car got a good look at me when I helped Silvair."

Sergei glared at Silvair furiously.

"Dis is vhy you change de color of de hair, ja?" Silvair asked uncomfortably.

She hadn't meant to make them feel guilty for something she'd chosen to do and she certainly hadn't intended to make them angry with one another. "Yes, and it'll probably work, especially since it was dark, and I don't intend to hang around here for long anyway. I figured, once I'd helped you two get away, I'd move north and find a quiet little town where nobody knows me. I'm sure I'll be fine now that Panas is dead. Eventually, I'll have to talk to the cops, but I think I can get out of any charges. I'm not sure you two could—Panas had surveillance cameras all over the place—and I don't want to see you go to jail. It isn't that I want you to go. I just think it'd be much better for both of you if you did."

To her relief, that seemed to pacify them. They relaxed visibly.

"Dey are looking for de lion and de tiger," Sergei said. "Dey never see Sergei or Silvair in de man-skin. We broked those machines dat take our picture."

A terrible sadness descended over her. "But that's who you really are, isn't it? Lion and tiger? You can't help but change and any time you're seen they're going to want to kill you or cage you."

Both men shrugged. "Dat is always de way of tings, no matter where we live," Sergei said.

She thought for a moment that she'd start crying. Maybe they could accept that as a way of life, but she didn't think she could—in fact she *knew* she couldn't. She'd never done anything in her life like she had when the cops had been scrambling to catch and/or kill them. She'd been desperate to protect them or she wouldn't have done it then.

And, if she had it to do over again, she would.

Apparently they saw how close to tears she was. They studied her uneasily for several moments and finally glanced at one another in that silent communication they shared so often. She wondered if they were even aware of the connection they'd formed with one another. She supposed they were. Despite the rivalry they'd displayed so often, they hadn't tried to kill one another and they were natural enemies, weren't they? Or was it different because they weren't actually all lion and tiger but part human, too?

Maybe it was just because they were both and there wasn't anyone else like them around?

"We go eat now, ja?" Silvair said abruptly. "Den we look around dis man-village."

She couldn't help but smile at the last comment even though she didn't particularly want to stroll around the city streets and risk getting into more trouble. "City," she corrected him. "I've never been here myself. I'd enjoy that."

They took her to a dine-in restaurant to Kate's surprise, not a very fancy, expensive one, but a nice restaurant, and she hadn't been taken out to dine in a restaurant in a very long time. Sergei looked as if he was excruciatingly uncomfortable, at least at first, although he tried hard to hide it. Silvair seemed surprisingly at home.

Sergei lost his self-consciousness about the place as soon as he was presented with a huge steak that was so rare it made Kate feel slightly unwell to watch the two of them eating the bloody things.

"What did you do before you came to this country?" she asked Silvair curiously.

"Sometime I live in de man-villages like dis one, sometime on de plain vhere I can roam free. I do one for a vhile and den de udder."

Kate flicked a glance around to make certain no one was close enough to overhear their conversation. "That's why you didn't have any trouble driving."

He nodded, although he looked mildly irritated that she seemed surprised he could drive. "Most all of de people do de same tings as man-children vhen dey live among them—den dey blend in. Vhen I live in de man-villages, I fix de man-machines—de cars—live in man-house, drive car, eat man-children food."

Kate blushed uncomfortably. "I'm sorry if that was insulting. It's just—I've never met ... never known ... anyone like you."

Amusement lit his eyes. "You tink. Me, I doan know dis place, doan know de man-speak here dat well, but dere ... dey doan know. Dey tink I'm just like dey are."

That was an unsettling piece of information, and she felt stupid for assuming they were 'one of a kind'. It wasn't even logical that they would be. They had to have parents, or at least have *had* them. They hadn't just magically appeared—she didn't suppose.

She frowned at that thought, wondering, but decided not to ask since she didn't want to risk insulting them again. Idly stirring the remains of her dinner around with the tines of her fork, she considered whether to ask the question uppermost in her mind and finally did. "You have family there?"

He shrugged. "De pride—dis is much like a family. My mate, she die long time ago. My son, he roam wid de pride dis year. Next year he go to university and learn de computer—speak." He frowned, obviously groping for the English words. "Build computers and make de program."

Kate blinked at him in surprise. Stunned, she supposed, more nearly described her feelings and not just because he had a son, or that son was going to the university to learn computer science, not even because it was hard to grasp, even after what he'd already told her, that they lived and worked among humans. He didn't look *old* enough to have a son old enough to go to college.

Grim amusement flickered in his eyes. "You tink dis feline dumb 'cause my speak so bad, eh?"

Kate reddened. Under the circumstances, it seemed better to voice her question than to let him think such a thing—which she didn't. She was more inclined to think he and Sergei were amazingly intelligent. "I think your English is terrible, and hard to follow sometimes, but I can't speak your language at all, so, no, I don't think you're dumb!" She actually thought their accents were adorable, but she didn't think they'd be very pleased about the fact that she thought it was 'cute'. "I was just thinking you don't look old enough to have a son in college."

He studied her assessingly for a moment, apparently decided she was telling the truth, and slid a glance in Sergei's direction, grinning. "Dis ol' lion younger dan dat ol' tiger dere, I'm tinking."

The 'old' tiger reddened, glaring at him. "I have tirty-seven summers, lion man," he growled. "How many you have?"

Silvair's grin broadened. "Tirty-five."

Sergei shrugged. He'd suspected as much. It irritated him to discover Silvair *was* younger than him almost as much as it annoyed him for Silvair to gloat about it. "Dat only two summers. You no young cub."

If she'd tried to guess, she wouldn't have figured either of them for much more than thirty, if that—not that that handful of years made that much difference. She wasn't about to tell Silvair she'd thought he was the oldest of the two, though, not when they were already taunting one another about it.

She also wasn't going to tell them her age. They could guess all they wanted to—but she was going to brain both of them if they guessed her older than she was.

Either they realized she wasn't comfortable with the age discussion or they just didn't care. Neither one of them asked.

She was almost more insulted about the fact that they weren't interested enough to ask.

"I guess you lived in the … uh … man-villages where you were from, too?" she asked Sergei, more because she wanted him to talk than because she expected his story would be any different.

He looked uncomfortable about the question. "Sometimes," he said evasively.

Kate wondered why he didn't want to talk about it and couldn't decide whether to pursue her questions or not. She *wanted* to know about him. She also didn't want him to think she didn't care to know when she'd asked Silvair so many questions. "Do you have a family there?"

"Nyet—no."

"Just the … uh … pride?"

His lips tightened. "Nyet."

Her throat closed. No one. He had no one and he didn't want to talk about it. She was a little hurt—more than a little, she acknowledged—that he didn't seem to want to tell her anything about himself. Obviously, he found it painful or at least uncomfortable to admit he was alone, or maybe he just felt like she must look down on him when he couldn't claim as much experience in the world of man as Silvair had?

She tried to clear her throat of the tightness there, searched her mind for something she could say that might make him feel less uncomfortable. "You seem to know a lot about cars, too," she finally said tentatively, although she hadn't noticed anything beyond the fact that he seemed fairly familiar with driving.

He regarded her with what she could only interpret as brooding violence. After a moment, though, he seemed to tamp his temper with an effort. "When I was boy, I make furniture wid my sire," he said finally.

There was something about the way he said it that warned her off, that told her he wouldn't welcome any probing at all. It seemed significant that he'd said 'when he was a boy'. Unspoken, was the insinuation that he hadn't done so since that time and she wondered why he hadn't. Something terrible, she felt certain, must have happened. "It must have been very satisfying to make things with your hands."

He seemed to relax fractionally, but his anger, or more specifically the deep hurt he was struggling to hide behind a wall of anger, crushed her spirits. She was relieved when they paid for their dinner and left to walk.

She thought idly … until they led her directly to a casino.

Chapter Fifteen

Fear was uppermost in Kate's mind when she discovered Sergei and Silvair fully intended to go in. Anger followed very quickly on the heels of it. She stopped walking as soon as she realized their destination. "We don't want to go into this place."

Silvair halted, turning to look at her in surprise. "Ve do. Ve gamble here, make more money, buy dat car. Is goot way to make wery much money."

"It's a good way to lose very much money," Kate contradicted tightly. "You'll end up losing everything you've got and then some—and you won't have money even to buy an old car then."

"You tink I doan know how to gamble?" Silvair asked, anger threading his voice.

She didn't care if he was angry, and she didn't care if he thought she was insulting his intelligence. "Nobody knows how to gamble, if you mean *win*! It's just blind luck and the house has all the luck!"

"Dis place make you afraid, Katie?" Sergei asked gruffly.

The understanding in his voice instantly transformed her anger into an urge to cry. She shook her head in denial.

Silvair's irritation vanished. "No mans here like dat Panas."

"How do you know that?" she demanded. "It could be somebody *just* like him that's running this place. Nice men don't get rich in this kind of business! It takes … ruthlessness. They use the lure of getting rich to bring people in to throw away every cent they've got—and sometimes *more* than they've got!

"That's how I ended up in Panas' clutches to begin with! I know you didn't believe me when I told you this, but it's true! My boyfriend gambled! He gambled his life away because he owed more money than he could possibly pay back and Panas threatened to kill me if I didn't work for him to pay off Jeff's debt!"

Sergei's face tightened with anger. "Why dis man of yours let Panas do dat to you? Why he doan pay his own debt?"

Kate sniffed, blinking back her tears with an effort. "Because he was dead! He was scared and he ran, but it didn't do him any good! Maybe he thought they wouldn't come after me. Maybe he just didn't care. I don't know, but I do know he wouldn't have gotten into such a mess to start with if he hadn't been convinced he could win if he just kept gambling."

The two men exchanged a look. "Ve take you back to de hotel," Silvair said decisively, taking her arm and guiding her back toward the street.

She knew from their expressions that they hadn't given up on the idea. They were just going to take her to the hotel and come back. She looked at them despairingly, but she couldn't think of anything to say to convince them if that hadn't. "We don't really need it. We can get by on what you have now. We could … borrow a car to make the trip out, or maybe take a bus."

"We talk about dis later," Sergei said gruffly.

"At the hotel?" Kate asked hopefully.

"Vhen ve get back," Silvair agreed.

Kate stopped. "I'd rather stay with you," she said. "I don't want to go back to the hotel yet."

They studied her with a mixture of doubt and irritation. "You doan want to go in dat place," Sergei said with obviously strained patience.

She pasted a tight smile on her face. "I changed my mind. I'd be bored at the hotel by myself."

"You vatch TV," Silvair suggested.

Like the news? She was afraid she'd see them on the news and that was why she didn't want to go back by herself. At least if she was with them she might be able to convince them not to do anything that would get them in jail. "This would be more interesting."

They wanted to take her back to the hotel. She could see they did. She could also see that they didn't actually want to argue with her about it—certainly not on the street—and they didn't have any idea of how they could resolve the situation to their satisfaction without hauling her up and carting her off. "I'll stay out of the way. I promise."

Shrugging, they turned toward the casino again, flanking her as they entered the building. They surprised her by not immediately heading for one off the slot machines or the tables. Instead, they strolled around and around the casino, pausing now and then to watch. She was beginning to relax fractionally and to hope that they didn't actually mean to gamble, that she'd entirely misunderstood their reason for going in, when she realized they'd only been studying the play.

Divide and conquer, she thought in dismay when she discovered Sergei had led her off in one direction while Silvair disappeared in another. When she finally realized he was no longer with them, she discovered he'd gone to get chips while Sergei distracted her.

Tension coiled in her stomach in a nauseating knot that made her regret the food she'd enjoyed earlier. If she hadn't been afraid of attracting unwanted attention and also been certain it wouldn't do any good at all, she would've considered creating a scene. She did consider it, briefly, but dismissed the idea on both grounds. It might get them all thrown out, but it also might get them arrested, and beyond that, there was nothing to stop either of them from finding another casino.

She hated gambling. She hated what it did to people and everyone around them for that matter. She would never have thought Sergei or Silvair was the type to want to gamble. In spite of everything that had happened, everything she knew they'd done, she'd still thought of them as 'good'. It wasn't that she wasn't horrified about them killing Panas and his men, but she knew damned well that had been a case of kill or be killed. She couldn't condemn them for that.

She especially couldn't find room to condemn them for doing something she'd wanted to do, had thought about doing, and would have done if she'd thought she could manage it *and* get away with it. Panas and his goons had definitely been on the 'needed killing' list and they hadn't harmed anyone else, even though they'd been chased and shot at.

They'd rescued her from a living hell and they'd taken such good care of her.

It made her sick to think they were going to lose the money they'd taken from Panas because she knew that was going to leave them with no recourse but to do something else illegal. And sooner or later, if they didn't leave, they were going to get into terrible trouble, or they were going to get killed.

She couldn't think of any way she could save them from themselves, though, nothing she could do but watch disaster unfold before her eyes.

And she still preferred that to waiting in the hotel and wondering what was happening.

Silvair rejoined them after a while, led her off to get a drink at the bar and Sergei disappeared. It took all she could do to pretend she was enjoying herself when she'd never been more miserable in her life.

Relief filled her when they finally decided to leave. It was short lived. Instead of turning toward the hotel, they headed for another casino.

It was a nightmare, she thought, that wasn't going to end until they'd lost everything—and maybe not even then.

Two hours later, the nightmare took a turn she'd never expected. When Silvair and Sergei met up with her to leave, they had four security men on their tails. The men detained the three of them and escorted them to a back office.

It was some relief that Sergei and Silvair had allowed themselves to be detained without instantly turning on the men. She'd more than half feared they would and knew if they did none of them would ever manage to make it out of the casino.

Sergei restlessly prowled the room where they'd been asked to wait to speak with the head of security, regretting the decision to allow Kate to stay with them. They should not have allowed her to know what they'd intended, should have known it was too risky for her. Neither of them had liked the idea of leaving her alone at the hotel, though.

They'd thought she would be safer with them.

They hadn't considered she'd be in the middle of any battle

they had to fight.

Silvair should have thought of it, he thought angrily. He was familiar with this kind of place, familiar enough he'd known the danger of winning too much money in one place. *He* had been careful. He could only conclude that Silvair hadn't been careful enough or they wouldn't have been detained for questioning.

He realized immediately what had happened when the head of the security finally arrived.

She paused in the door to survey the three of them through narrowed eyes, then turned to one of the security guards standing by the door. "Kurt, why don't escort Ms ....?"

Kate merely stared at the woman, feeling hostility instantly rise inside of her.

When she didn't answer, the woman's face hardened. "... The woman to another room."

"She stays with us!" Sergei growled.

The woman turned to him when he spoke, scanning him in a leisurely manner that missed nothing. Despite her air of professionalism, Kate didn't miss the purely feminine interest in the woman's eyes and she didn't like it one little bit.

The woman shrugged and turned to her security men. "You can wait outside while I talk to them."

They looked reluctant, but finally left. "We'll be right outside, Ms. Cantrell," the last man to leave informed them, the one she'd called Kurt.

Ms. Cantrell didn't even acknowledge him. She was too busy molesting Silvair and Sergei with her gaze. "Is she your woman?" she asked when the door shut, studying Sergei speculatively.

Sergei and Silvair both turned to study her.

"Da."

"Ja."

Cantrell frowned, glancing from one man to the other when they answered her. "Which?"

Sergei and Silvair glared at one anther balefully.

Cantrell's lips tightened. "She's a man-child!"

Bemused already that Sergei and Silvair had *both* claimed

her as their woman when she'd had no inkling either one of them would, Kate felt her jaw drop at that comment. "You're …?"

Cantrell folded her arms over her chest. Ignoring Kate, she focused on the men, or more specifically, Sergei, speaking to him in what Kate supposed was Russian. "You don't belong to the local tribe or you'd know this club is off-limits to any of our people. It's under my protection."

The comment diverted Sergei from his contemplation of choking the life out of Silvair.

Kate hadn't understood anything the woman had said, but she decided she didn't particularly care for the speculative interest in his eyes.

"Dis club is tribe lands?" he asked slowly.

Cantrell's lips tightened when he spoke to her in English instead of responding in Russian. She turned to look at Kate. "You may trust the man-child. I don't." She shifted into Russian again and then repeated whatever she'd said in German for Silvair's benefit. "I won't discuss clan business in her presence. You've been warned. Take your winnings and go. If I see either of you here again, though, you may be certain you'll be brought before the council."

Sergei and Silvair exchanged a long look.

"Dare are udder clubs ve are not to wisit?" Silvair asked.

Cantrell shrugged and gave them the name of another casino.

She stopped them as the three of them reached the door, again speaking first to Sergei in Russian and then to Silvair in German. "If you two are only passing through, then make your visit short. If you plan on lingering, or have an interest in becoming a clan member, you'll need to meet with the head of the clan. Contact me and I'll set up a meeting." She paused. "You two are bloods, aren't you, were-humans not were-feline?" She didn't wait for either of them to respond. "We don't have any other members that are, but I'm certain you'd be welcome to join our clan … so long as you're willing to abide by clan law. When it comes down to it, we're all felines, right?"

Sergei frowned, but he had no intention of committing himself until he'd had time to consider it. She seemed to sense his reluctance.

"We have a large, well established network here in the U.S. Why sully your lines with the man-child? If you're looking for mates, there are plenty of females available, tigress and lioness—if you want pure lines."

* * * *

Kate was relieved when they were escorted from the casino and released, at least of the anxiety of death, dismemberment, or jail. It was embarrassing to be shown the door—people noticed—but a little public embarrassment beat the hell out of being arrested, or worse.

She was still disturbed about the entire incident, but mostly because Cantrell was were-feline and she'd made no bones about the fact that she found both Sergei and Silvair very much to her liking.

Neither man was inclined to be talkative at the best of times, and she knew their silence alone wasn't necessarily an indication that anything that might disturb her was going on, but she felt … threatened by the fact that the woman had deliberately spoken to them in their native languages. She knew part of that was merely a means of preventing *her* from knowing what the subject under discussion was. She suspected, though, that it was *also* to impress both Sergei and Silvair.

She just wasn't as sure as she would've liked to be that it hadn't.

"She's … one of you?" she asked finally when she couldn't contain herself any more, even though she didn't particularly want to let them know it was bothering her.

Sergei grunted in response.

"She is panther," Silvair said absently.

Kate frowned when her opening gambit didn't provide her with any more information than that. "What happened?" she asked after they'd walked another block in silence.

Sergei glanced at her absently. "Dey let us go."

Kate's lips tightened in irritation. "Why did they want to

speak to you in the first place?"

"Dey knew ve vas cheating," Silvair said unconcernedly.

Kate's jaw dropped in stunned disbelief. "You were cheating?" she gasped, horrified.

Sergei shrugged. "We use our feline senses. We hear and see tings de man-child can't."

Kate digested that during the rest of the walk back to the hotel. "That wasn't cheating," she disputed indignantly once they were safely inside their room where no one could overhear. Both men looked at her blankly, which wasn't surprising, she supposed since a good twenty minutes had passed since they'd spoken a word, but she *suspected* that the reason they had no idea what she was referring to was because they hadn't been listening to her to start with. And she suspected the reason they'd been so quiet and absentminded was because their minds were on that—female! "Using your senses," she elaborated. "Everyone else does. Why is it cheating only because *yours* are better?"

Sergei studied her with a mixture of surprise and amusement. "Because these tings are made for de man-children. We have an unfair advantage."

"Says who!" Kate demanded. "There wasn't a sign on the door that said 'no were-felines allowed'! I can't *believe* they had the nerve to throw us out only because *that woman* decided you were cheating!"

Silvair chuckled. "You did not like dat feline, Sveety?"

Kate sniffed. "Not especially, no."

"I doan tink she like you neider," Sergei murmured, his eyes gleaming with amusement.

Kate glared at him angrily but found herself abruptly struggling with the urge to cry. She swallowed with an effort against the ball of anger and misery congesting her chest and closing her throat. "I think I'll take a shower," she said.

She turned on the shower when she'd locked the bathroom door firmly behind her, but instead of getting in, she sat down on the edge of the tub and covered her face with her hands, trying to figure out why she felt the need to cry.

Nerves, she told herself. It had upset her to go into the

casinos, fearing Silvair and Sergei would only get into more trouble. It had scared her when the security men had taken them in to talk to the head of security, and that was another very good reason to feel like crying her eyes out.

If that was the real reason she felt like crying, though, why was it her mind kept going back to the way *that woman* had looked Sergei and Silvair over as if they were two choice pieces of steak? Why was it that she kept remembering the way they'd looked back at her with interest? Why was it that she kept trying to convince herself that they *hadn't* looked at that hateful Cantrell woman with interest?

It was just because she was one of them, she decided. She wasn't even pretty—not especially pretty, anyway, just sort of ordinary, really.

Except even she had noticed the woman had a knock out figure. She didn't believe for a moment that neither Silvair or Sergei hadn't noticed *that*. It was probably all they'd noticed besides the fact that she was one of them—and she could speak their language.

It occurred to Kate after a while that she had no idea how long she'd been holed up in the bathroom 'taking a shower'. If she stayed too long she might just as well have broken down and cried in front of them because they were going to know she was upset.

She hadn't yielded to the urge because she'd been afraid they'd hear her and they'd notice her swollen eyes and red nose. She still felt crying because she hadn't managed to work up a healthy dose of resentment and anger. She ached with the need to release the pent up tears, but she wasn't going to give in to it.

It was bad enough *that woman* was prettier than her, had a better figure, was one of them, and spoke their language. There was no way she was going to make herself look even less appealing by crying all over them and no surer way to make them start looking for an excuse to leave again.

If they wanted to sneak off in the middle of the night to go see the damned bitch, there was nothing she could do to stop them, but she wasn't going to give them an excuse to rub her nose in it.

Shutting off the tub—which was when she realized she'd never actually gotten around to switching it to the shower—she went to the lavatory to bathe her face in cool water until the sense of imminent loss of control receded and then left the bathroom.

She could sense both Sergei and Silvair studying her intently, although she didn't look at either one of them—which was when she realized she'd never gotten around to taking her clothes off either. Releasing a pent up sigh of self-disgust, she kicked her tennis shoes off, peeled her jeans off, and crawled into the bed in her panties and t-shirt.

If they said anything—and she doubted they would—she would just tell them she'd had too much to drink. She *had* sipped on a mixed drink at the bar. They had no way of knowing how much it took to make her tipsy.

The dip of the bed on first one side and then the other woke her from a sound sleep. As disoriented as she was, still more asleep than awake, she inched closer to the chest nearest her face and nuzzled against him, breathing deeply. No stray feline scent there. Rolling over, she nuzzled against Silvair and tested him for any unfamiliar scent. Satisfied when she didn't detect one, she drifted to sleep again.

* * * *

A pervasive sense of doom invaded Kate as soon as she began to drift toward awareness. She lay as she was for a while, struggling to sink back into unconsciousness to avoid examining the blanket of depression too closely but discovered that even though she couldn't actually identify the reason for it, she couldn't evade it altogether and find sleep again.

The water was running in the bathroom. It wasn't the shower, she decided, but the lavatory faucet, and an image of Silvair or Sergei standing at the sink shaving rose in her mind. With her eyes still closed, she expanded her senses beyond the bed, which was empty except for her, to the room around her. Deciding no one was in the room with her, she lifted her head and peered around through narrowed, burning eyes to verify that fact and collapsed again when she saw she was right.

The water was shut off at the lavatory sink. She lifted one eyelid just high enough to identify the owner of the tread she heard leaving the bathroom and saw that it was Sergei. Wondering where Silvair was, she dragged herself from the bed and headed into the bathroom.

The long, hot shower she took roused her sluggish brain a few levels in alertness, but it didn't chase away the sense of misery clinging to her like a black cloud. Mopping the fog from the bathroom mirror when she got out, she studied her glum reflection a few moments, sighed, and focused on brushing her teeth.

Still wrapped in her towel, she left the bathroom a few minutes later, wondering if she could find a place to do laundry or, alternately, if they didn't have time for it, if she could bum enough money from one of the guys to go back to the second hand shop for a couple more changes of clothing.

Sergei, wearing nothing but his jeans, which she noticed he hadn't bothered to fasten, was sitting up in the bed with his back propped against the headboard when she came out. She felt his gaze on her, but she didn't look directly at him as she sorted halfheartedly through her clothes.

"Kate?"

Frowning, she refused to look at him as she tucked a t-shirt and panties under her arm and studied the jeans she'd picked up to see if it was the clean pair or the ones she'd worn the day before. "What?"

"Come here."

Reluctance immediately shot through her, but she glanced at him and, after a moment, moved to the bed. He took the clothes she'd tucked under her arm and tossed them toward the other side of the bed without glancing in that direction. Catching the tuck of the towel, he tugged it off as he pulled her closer.

She didn't try to resist. When he caught her waist and dragged her up onto the bed and across his lap, she placed a knee on either side of his hips and met his gaze.

Chapter Sixteen

Beyond the heated tumult of passion there was a question in Sergei's eyes as he studied her that Kate didn't want to answer even if she could've, and she wasn't certain she knew the answer he was looking for. The gathering of chaotic, painful emotion inside of her that vied with the warming tide of desire in response to what she saw his eyes was answer enough, she supposed.

Impending, painful loss.

She recognized the feeling even though she firmly refused to examine it too closely. Closing her eyes against the sting in her eyes in response, she swallowed against the painful tightening in her throat and lifted her lips to him in mute invitation. His breath, a harsh exhalation as if he'd been holding it, puffed against her lips a moment before the heat of his mouth covered them, drinking in her own sigh that was part relief he hadn't voiced the question in his eyes, but mostly welcome.

His arms tightened around her, bringing her close enough the tips of her breasts brushed against his hard male breasts and blood rushed to her nipples in response. Sliding one arm upward to her shoulder blades and one down to her buttocks, he pulled her closer still as he stroked his tongue over hers in an almost lazy caress.

Hot moisture gathered in her eyes and dampened her lashes at the measured stroke of his tongue along hers and the gentleness of his hold, at the elixir of his taste and scent that filled her with a desperate yearning that was only partly passion. She needed savage possession that left no room for anything beyond the mindlessness of primal, carnal need, she knew, or the tears gathering determinedly in her eyes would escape the dam of her lashes.

Gliding her palms from his shoulders to his back, she

clasped him more tightly to her and sucked on his tongue. A shudder went through him in response. His arms tightened briefly and then he shifted down in the bed until he could press her damp cleft against his lower belly. The fragile flesh clung briefly and parted from him with the rhythmic pressure of his palm against her buttocks, teasing the sensitive folds and stirring warmth to heat. His lips clung to hers more tightly. His tongue became more insistent, more demanding, the two together more eloquent of rising hunger.

The hot tears that had gathered in her eyes bridged the dam of her lashes, escaping to trail down her cheeks, but the urge receded as her need kept pace with his, the growing, throbbing ache in her sex usurping the tightness in her chest. Urging her to rise up, he reached between them to stroke her cleft and tease the engorged bud at the apex briefly before grasping his turgid flesh and aligning it with her cleft. He pressed down on her hips again to nestle his flesh firmly along her cleft, shifting her hips so that she rocked back and forth along the hot, tumescent flesh.

A trembling urgency had replaced the careful caresses he'd begun with. Dragging his lips from hers as he caught her arms and drew her upward, he wound a path from her lips to her breasts as he brought her to her knees and thereby her breasts within his reach. Steadying her with one arm around her, he tugged impatiently at first one erect nipple and then the other as he grasped his cock with his other hand and dragged it along her cleft to align their bodies and pressed inside of her.

She gasped, dropping her forehead to his broad shoulder at the delicious impalement, panting as his thick shaft, plowing relentlessly along her channel, produced a pleasurable ache that grew more pronounced as she lifted and settled until she could feel the head of his cock pressing almost painfully against her womb. She wanted him deeper still, needed to claim every inch of him. Spreading her thighs wider, she sank down on him until she could feel the faint abrasion of the nest of hair around the root of his cock brush lips of her sex and pain warred with pleasure.

He tightened his arms around her hips as if he felt the same need, breathing harsh pants of breath as he held her still for several heartbeats. Lifting one hand after a moment, he grasped her cheeks, forcing her face up—she thought to kiss her. Instead he paused. Sensing his gaze, she lifted her eyelids with an effort and stared back at him.

Consternation was clear in his expression. Doubt filled his eyes. Releasing his grip on her chin, he settled his palm on one cheek, stroking his thumb over the moisture he'd discovered.

Holding his gaze, she lifted slowly and settled again. He caught her hips to still her movements. "Did I hurt you, Katie?"

Not yet, she thought, but he was going to. Instead of answering, she moved closer, brushing her lips lightly along his as she shook her head. His hold on her eased. She lifted again, nipping at his lips in demand as she settled, taking him deeply inside of her.

He caught her face between his palms, kissing her until the heated hunger rose between them again. Abruptly, he released her, coiled his arms tightly around her and rolled with her until she was beneath him. Seizing control of the depth of penetration and the pace, he began to pump his hips in escalating rhythm that drew sighs of pleasure from her, then sharp gasps and moans as the stroke of his cock along the walls of her sex brought her closer and closer to culmination.

A quake rippled through her. She tilted her hips on the next downward stroke and caught the wave, tensing all over as her climax hit her and her body began to convulse with ecstatic spasms. He began to move faster as her cries sharpened until he was driving into her almost frenziedly. Abruptly, he froze. A jolt rippled through his big body. He uttered a choked groan as the first convulsion went through him, jerking with the force of each successive paroxysm until his body stopped seizing. A long, drawn out breath of relief escaped him.

Sated and weak in the aftermath, it took a concentrated effort to move, but, reluctant to give up her connection with him, Kate clung determinedly and finally began to stroke his back in a leisurely caress as he hovered above her, trying to gather the strength to move away, she knew. When he finally did, settling on his side beside her, she rolled toward him, nestling her cheek against his chest.

She felt surprise ripple through him, but after a moment he settled an arm around her. She waited for the lethargy of repletion to claim him—in vain. The tension didn't leave him and she knew he was debating whether to question her or not. Wry amusement filled her as she imagined the thoughts running through his head. Cut up his peace, now, when all he wanted to do was sleep, or wait for the axe to fall?

He released a harsh breath. "Why did you cry if I didn't hurt you?"

She hadn't actually expected him to take the plunge. It was unfortunate that she wasn't prepared. "I don't know," she responded, with perfect truth since she'd resolutely refused to examine it. "Maybe it's just close to my time of the month."

There was a strange look on his face when she pulled away to look up at him. Interpreting it, rightly or not, to mean he wasn't that familiar with the pre, mid, and post menstrual emotional rollercoaster, she shook her head instead of trying to explain it and rolled away from him. "Never mind. It just goes with the territory."

Gathering her clothes, she climbed off the other side of the bed and headed into the bathroom to clean up.

"Where's Silvair?" she asked when she emerged a few minutes later. "Gone to get food, I hope."

Sergei was sitting up against the headboard once more, his jeans still open to reveal his lower belly and the nest of hair there, although he'd tucked his cock back into them. Clearly neither man really cared to wear clothes at all. Despite the fact that she'd managed to collect shirts and shoes, they didn't put on either unless they left the room and rarely fastened or zipped the jeans they *did* wear.

"He has gone to buy de car. If he doan bring back food, we will go when he returns," he responded slowly after studying her keenly for several moments.

Kate looked at him in surprise. "He picked out a car?"

"Da. We did yesterday. He go to take de money to de man."

Kate stared at him, but finally decided against asking him which car. All of the cars Silvair had called about were late model, virtually new, and damned expensive. Either they'd won more money the night before than she'd thought possible, or ....

She didn't want to think about the 'or'.

Moving to one of the chairs, she plopped down on the seat and stared at the TV screen when Sergei turned it on. "We're leaving today?" she asked finally.

"Da," Sergei responded without elaborating.

The depression that had lifted briefly descended again. This time it was impossible to ignore the reason for it, or the flicker of relief that mingled with it.

She was glad they wouldn't be hanging around long enough for Silvair and Sergei to get to know *that woman* any better and depressed for the same reason because it meant, in two days, tops, she'd be parting company with them herself.

It was for the best, for all concerned, she told herself impatiently. They'd be safely away from the possibility of prosecution and she wouldn't be tempted to make another stupid mistake. Granted, they seemed to be better at gambling than poor Jeff had been, but it was enough that they seemed drawn to the same vice. She'd been mildly contemptuous of people addicted to it *before* Panas. She despised everything and everyone connected to it now.

Not Sergei or Silvair, yet, but she knew she'd learn to if she stayed around them long and watched it gain a stronger and stronger hold on them.

It was just as well there'd be no chance for her to become more deeply attached to them.

Dragging her legs up to the seat, she hooked her heels on the edge and locked her arms around her knees, folding into herself unconsciously. "We should probably stop somewhere and get a map," she said after a few moments.

Frowning, Sergei flicked a puzzled glance at her before training his gaze on the flickering screen again. He had no idea what was on the TV, nor did he care. He'd merely turned it on to try to drown the uncomfortable silence between them.

He was certain that, somehow, he'd hurt Kate. He just wasn't sure of how—not physically, although he'd been worried, at first, that he had. She'd seemed distressed the night before, though, he realized, not just angry.

He'd been inclined to dismiss the anger. He knew she hadn't liked them going into the casino. He regretted it. At the same time, he and Silvair had agreed it was the best, and certainly the fastest, way to come up with the money they figured they'd need to see her safely settled somewhere. He figured even if she hadn't liked the way they'd done it, she would get over it once she understood why they'd done it.

He was reluctant to tell her why, though, particularly considering the strange mood she'd been in since.

Was it only because it was her woman's time, he wondered?

He didn't know anything about it—not with regards to a man-child—and not a whole lot more, he acknowledged wryly, when it came to females of his own kind. His father hadn't been terribly forthcoming. Beyond informing him that he would 'sense' when a female was ready for mating and know it instantly for what it was—which he had with Kate, which had surprised him—and that 'the rest' would come to him naturally—which it had—thankfully—he didn't know a damned thing.

He had his doubts Silvair knew a hell of a lot more, for all his airs of being so much more experienced. He damned well wasn't going to ask him, particularly when, from what he could tell, Silvair was just as puzzled by Kate's behavior as he had been.

The dim memory of his childhood sweetheart was no help. *She* had been a man-child, but not even in the first blush of womanhood if he was to go by her father's furious diatribe when he'd caught them together. In any case, time wasn't the only thing that had dimmed those memories. He had worked hard to push them from his mind and the nightmare of finding himself responsible for the murder of his parents had overshadowed pretty much everything that had gone before and many, many years afterward.

Silvair came in while he was still trying to decide if he had enough command of her language to try to fish the information out of Kate since she didn't appear to be inclined to clear up the mystery for him. He caught the lingering scent from their coupling instantly, bristling almost visibly. Without a word, he dropped the keys he'd been twirling in his hand as he came in and made a beeline toward Kate.

Fury washed through Sergei as he watched his rival drag her into his embrace and remove *his* scent to replace it with his own. He tensed at the challenge as Silvair walked her to the wall, stripping her clothes from her as he went, but they'd challenged and counter challenged one another since they'd dragged Kate off with them and he forced himself to relax and ignore it as he had every time before, and for the same reason.

They were both well aware that they couldn't do battle for her without risking injury to her. She didn't have the strength or the reflexes of a female of their own kind and if they allowed themselves to get caught up in the heat of battle they couldn't be certain that they'd be able to ignore the urge to shift. Neither of them had wanted her to discover what they were in the beginning, which had been part of the reason they'd refrained, but mostly it had been because they both knew their instincts would control them once they shifted, not the reasoning side of their mind.

Resentment lingered, despite his iron grip on his temper, but as he watched Silvair guide his cock into her sex, desire shot through him, making him hard all over again. The temptation to watch, and then to take her again as soon as Silvair withdrew nearly overwhelmed his good sense for many minutes. Finally, disgusted with himself, he rose from the bed and went in the bathroom to cool the heat with the shower.

Fragile, he reminded himself, shivering as the cold water slid over his heated skin. They were pushing her to her limits as it was, each of them vying to mark her with his scent. No doubt the hike hadn't helped, nor the fact that they'd had difficulty finding food suitable for her, and could not afford to spare much time for her to rest, but she could not be accustomed to having two men rutting her constantly, let alone two such as he and Silvair.

She was no match for them both, and, deep down, he knew neither of them had any business pursuing this.

Cantrell had been clearly interested in both of them. He summoned the woman's image. She wasn't hard on the eyes, in fact far from it, and she'd sweetened the pot by suggesting there were many others. He felt a spark of interest in the possibility of finding others like himself, or at least feline, but it wasn't much more than a glimmer and it didn't go beyond the mild curiosity of wondering what it would be like to become a member of the clan.

He didn't give a fuck about his bloodlines. He couldn't find an ounce of interest in looking elsewhere for a mate. He wanted Kate.

Unfortunately, he was fairly certain that Silvair was just as determined to have her and just as unwilling to settle for anyone else.

* * * *

Kate was clearly favorably impressed with the car. Despite the animosity he'd felt toward Silvair for bathing her in his scent last, he exchanged a pleased grin with the lion man as she looked the car over with obvious approval.

"It's beautiful!" she said in that husky voice of hers that always stirred something pleasant in his belly. "It looks almost new. God! It must have been expensive."

He saw the flicker of anxiety in her eyes and glanced at Silvair again.

"Doan worry, Katie. I got goot deal," Silvair responded firmly.

She smiled at both of them tremulously and his enjoyment of seeing it was only slightly marred by the fact that he'd had to share that smile. Then again, he supposed it was only fair considering they'd each paid half.

"You should be able to get most of your money back when you sell it," she added after a few moments.

"It's yours, Katie," he said gruffly. "We smash yours. We get you anudder one."

Her lips parted in a breathless look of surprise and he

yielded to the impulse to cover her mouth with his own in a kiss that was deeply satisfying, however brief, because she responded instantly. She blushed when he released her, glancing self-consciously up and down the street, but then moved to Silvair and kissed him, as well. "Thank you, both," she said when she pulled away. "But I can't let you do this. This car is way nicer than the one I had. And, anyway, you'll need the money yourselves."

Sergei frowned, doubt instantly replacing his pleasure of moments before. "You doan like de car, Katie?"

"I love it! It's beautiful! It's just … too much for you to spend on me."

He exchanged a helpless look with Silvair, wondering how they were going to convince her to keep it if she didn't want it.

"I tell de man to put it in your name," Silvair said, pulling out the title. "Me an' Sergei doan need de car."

"Oh," Kate said, staring at the title. Her face reddened, but Sergei was damned if he knew why. She cleared her throat. "I should probably write my last name on this, too—just in case we get stopped and have to show the cops the title."

Finding a pen in the glove box, she wrote her name on it and shoved both the pen and the title back inside, closing it.

"Why don't one of you drive?" she suggested, handing the keys back to Silvair when he gave them to her. "I think you'll both be more comfortable in the front with your long legs, and I'm fine in the back."

Shrugging, Silvair glanced at Sergei questioningly. Sergei responded with a shrug of his own and climbed into the passenger seat. He didn't especially care to drive. He thought he did well enough considering he hadn't had a good deal of practice, but he didn't like the crowded streets of the city. He would actually have preferred to climb into the backseat with Kate, but he was fairly certain it would be too much temptation. It was still bothering the hell out of him that he could smell Silvair's scent on her skin and he was pretty sure that, by the time he'd replaced it with his own, he wouldn't want to stop at that.

They stopped to eat before they left the city and after a

couple of hours driving, Kate dozed off in the backseat.

"What did you tink of dat Cantrell?" Sergei asked when he was sure Kate was asleep.

Silvair slid a speculative look at him, glanced toward Kate, and then shrugged. "Purty female. She like your looks, I tink."

Sergei's lips tightened. "She like you more, I'm tinking."

Again, Silvair shrugged. "She wanted fucking. I doan mine dat, but I doan much like de panther. Dat kinda woman, she always want her own way. She too much like de man-children anyways. I'm tinking she not but half, maybe, especially de way she keep talkin' 'bout bloodlines. She was way more interested in de cub she get off dis lion dan dis ol' lion."

Sergei was silent for several moments. "You tink de clan a beeg clan?"

"She talked dat vay," Silvair responded. "Doan mean it is, but it beeger dan vhat dare vas vhere you vas from, ja? You tinking 'bout dem tigress she tell you 'bout?"

He had. He hadn't found the idea particularly tempting, but it was something to consider. He *needed* a mate. He wanted Kate, but that didn't mean she wanted him. For that matter, she might not want Silvair. They weren't man-children and even though she hadn't acted like it had bothered her to discover what they were, it didn't necessarily follow that she would be open to the possibility of allowing either one of them to claim her.

She hadn't disputed their claim to the panther woman, but that didn't mean anything either. Kate rarely voiced her objections. She just waited for the opportunity to do what she wanted without opposition.

"You tol' me you vant to find more of de people. You tinking 'bout settling dere and joinin' dat dere clan after ve get Kate settled somevhere vhere she be safe?"

Instead of answering directly, Sergei shrugged. "I tink I won't go back to de ol' country."

"I tink I won't neider," Silvair said.

Stalemate—again. Silvair wasn't giving up on Kate, either, and sooner or later they were going to battle it out over her—and probably both end up looking like fools. He might not know a hell of a lot about them, but he did know man-children didn't settle such things that way. Kate would probably take off the moment they tied up and then refuse to have anything to do with either one of them.

* * * *

It took all Kate could do to pretend to still be asleep.

She wondered if she'd heard the entire conversation or only the tail end of it. It had been the drone of their deep voices, though, that had woken her, and she supposed she must have heard it all.

Not that that mattered one way another. She'd heard enough even if she hadn't heard all of it.

Enough to realize why she'd been so depressed ... because she wasn't surprised. Somewhere in the back of her mind she must have realized meeting up with the Cantrell woman meant Sergei and Silvair had found an enclave of their own people. She knew they hadn't known Cantrell, or expected what had happened when they'd been pulled in by security, but she couldn't help but wonder if they'd had some idea about the feline people being in the area and if that was why they'd gone to Las Vegas to begin with.

Not that that mattered either. The bottom line was that they'd found their own people and they were going to take her off and dump her like an unwanted puppy.

That was why she'd felt like crying her eyes out the night before. They'd let her tag along. They hadn't minded fucking her senseless whenever the mood struck them, but they didn't really want her.

That was why she hadn't been able to hold the tears back when she'd made love to Sergei, because she knew it was the beginning of the end—even when she'd made that pathetic offering in hopes that he'd still want her, thinking if she made love to him he'd feel what she felt, she'd known he was already looking ahead to the time when she wouldn't be underfoot anymore.

No doubt *that woman* had offered them jobs in the casino. That was what the bitch had been talking so cozily to them about when she'd made sure *she* couldn't understand. Inviting them to join the clan, offering them jobs—and none too subtle hints that she was available.

If there was one thing she *did* know, it was men, and men weren't big on subtly, either using it or picking up on it. If they'd figured out the bitch was offering herself, she'd been damned blatant about it!

She had figured it out really quickly, but then she was a woman. All she'd had to see was the way Cantrell looked them over like she wanted to lick them and she'd known the woman was interested—even without the posturing she'd done to flaunt her sexy body.

Realizing abruptly that she was pushing herself closer and closer to bursting into tears with her unhappy thoughts, she tried to divert her mind to more positive things—like what she was going to do after they dumped her in some 'safe' place.

She might have felt better about them being worried enough about her to want to make sure she was safe except she thought they were just that way—just naturally protective. As big and rough and tough as they were, they'd always been careful of her, even from the beginning. They hadn't *grown* protective and careful so that she could see it as a possible growing attachment to her.

No, she was the one who'd grown attached. She should've seen it coming, but by the time she'd realized she was wrong to believe they meant her any harm, it was already too late.

Firmly quashing those depressing thoughts, she considered where they might be taking her—north, she supposed, since she'd been stupid enough to mention she thought that was what she'd do. They didn't know the country. Maybe they just figured they'd drive far enough she wasn't likely to find her way back?

Not that she dared even if she'd thought there was a chance in hell going back would make any difference at all. Her circumstances hadn't taken a turn for the better, even if theirs had. She still had to worry about the possibility that some of Panas' men might see her, or come looking for her. *Two* of them had still been alive when Silvair and Sergei had come barreling out of the club. They might still not have survived the attack, or they might have been hurt badly enough the cops grabbed them when they arrived, but she couldn't count on being completely safe from them. There might have been other survivors, if it came to that. She hadn't gotten the chance to find out any of the news on the story—it was 'old' news by the time they'd reached the city and if there'd been anything about it in the local news at the time, they'd already moved on to fresher stories.

Like the two great cats spotted in the city that had eluded capture.

Deciding after a while that she'd feigned sleep long enough to avoid suspicion, Kate sat up and stared out the window, trying to find something to divert her mind from the desolate thoughts that kept rambling around and around in her head.

Chapter Seventeen

Kate was so distracted by her bleak thoughts that it was a while before it dawned on her that she could confront them about their destination without giving away the fact that she'd been eavesdropping—and *boy* had her grandmother ever been right about that!

Eavesdroppers never hear good things about themselves!

Not that she hadn't learned that lesson long ago, and she hadn't intentionally snooped on their conversation anyway. She'd just woken at the wrong time and she'd been too uncomfortable to let them know she'd heard.

The sign saying they were leaving the state of Nevada and entering Idaho was too blatant to ignore, though. If she didn't say anything they were bound to realize she'd heard their conversation when she wasn't surprised. "We're going north?"

Silvair, who'd changed places with Sergei after they'd stopped to eat, swiveled around to look at her. "Ve tought ve vould take you to a safe place vhere you not have to vorry 'bout de bad mans."

It was hard not to look dismayed even though it wasn't a surprise. "But … I thought I was going to help you two get to the coast."

Silvair studied her. "Ve not goin' to de coast," he said finally.

"You're not?" she prompted.

"Nyet," Sergei said flatly, ignoring her invitation to share.

Not that she was surprised, but it did make her feel rebuffed anyway. "Where are you taking me?" she managed to ask after a few moments.

"You tell us vhen you see place you like, ja?"

"Oh—I get to choose?" she asked, struggling to keep the venom out of her voice and plastering a bright smile on her face when Silvair glanced at her sharply. She met Sergei's gaze in the mirror briefly as he glanced back at her, but looked away. "I was actually thinking about someplace in Idaho. I grew up there—in the state. I haven't been back since my grandma died, and I don't really want to go back to my hometown, but I like the area."

Chicken shit, she mentally berated herself. "It's really thoughtful of you to do this, but you really didn't have to. I've been on my own for a while now. I could've managed."

She flicked a glance at them, but it was already getting dark and hard to tell anything about their expressions. "You could just put me on a bus … if you've got somewhere in particular to go, I mean."

They didn't take the bait, damn them!

"Ve go vid you," Silvair said firmly. "Make sure everyting alright first."

"Oh! That's so sweet … and so completely unnecessary."

"*Is* necessary," Sergei contradicted.

She bit her tongue, refusing to give in to the urge to say something really ugly. Why make things worse? They were going to do what they wanted to, regardless of what she said. The only effect being a bitch was going to have was to make them want to go more, and faster, and it wouldn't make her feel a damned bit better.

And she didn't *want* them to leave her. She might not be able to convince them to stay no matter what she did, but she could sure as hell convince them to leave.

The anger didn't last nearly long enough to sustain her anyway. Depression set in the moment she accepted she couldn't change things. She was a 'man-child' and they weren't. They wanted, naturally enough, to be with their kind. For the sake of her pride, she did her best to pretend she was pleased at the prospect, even though she couldn't summon the energy to act as if she was excited. She was a twisted mass of raw emotions by the time they stopped for the night and she realized they were probably going to turn around and head back the following day.

She made love to them. She'd discovered all she really had to do was stroll through the room half naked to entice them.

She didn't even have to be completely naked and, thankfully, that hadn't changed.

She even managed to get through making love to both of them without bursting into tears and squalling like a baby.

She did that afterwards in the shower where they couldn't hear her.

They were gone when she woke up the following morning, which gave her the luxury of crying her eyes out for a solid hour before she exhausted herself and fell asleep again. She was lying on the bed with a cold compress over her swollen eyes when they returned late in the afternoon.

Stunned, she sat up in the bed and gaped at them while their grins slowly fell and their brows came together in puzzled frowns. "You are sick?" Sergei asked uneasily.

Feeling like kicking herself, Kate managed a wan smile. "Just a little headache," she mumbled.

The two men exchanged an uncertain glance. "Come," Silvair said finally. "Ve show you someting make you feel better."

"Maybe eat first?" Sergei asked. "You hungry, Katie? Maybe de headache go way if you eat, da?"

Heartened by the fact that they apparently weren't in as big a hurry to dump her and leave as she'd thought, she managed a brighter smile. "I think, maybe, that's it," she said. "I haven't eaten yet today."

Anger replaced the worry in Sergei's eyes. "Why you no eat, Katie?"

She reddened. "I just didn't feel eating," she said a little testily.

They hustled her off to the local diner to eat. She actually did feel better afterwards, but she thought it was only partly because of the food.

When they left the diner, they took a narrow road leading north out of town. They drove for about thirty minutes and finally turned off on an even narrower switch back road. It led to a small cabin.

Shutting the car off, Sergei and Silvair got out, their expressions pleased as they looked around. Uneasy about stopping in someone's front yard, Kate got out more slowly.

"Dis is nice place," Sergei said enthusiastically, dropping an arm across her shoulders and leading her to the edge of the clearing around the house so that she could look at the view.

"It's ... breathtaking," Kate agreed.

"Come see de house," Silvair said. "Need work, but is goot solid house. Sergei look at it goot and he know dis ting."

"Da. No wood rot," Sergei agreed, guiding her back toward the cabin. "Not a beeg place, but it be good when fix up a leedle bit. Got electric. Got well and septic. An' we got enough money left to fix dis place good."

Their enthusiasm was contagious but confusing. Bemused, Kate allowed them to lead her into the house and stared at everything they pointed out. Slowly, it congealed in her mind that they'd bought it—for her.

And they were so pleased with themselves!

And they had enough money left over to fix it up.

They'd gone to the casino to get money for her, she realized abruptly. She'd thought all sorts of awful things about them and they'd only done it for her!

She couldn't help it. She struggled with the urge a moment and finally burst into tears.

"You doan like it, Katie?" Sergei demanded gruffly. "We go back to de man and get de money back."

"I tol' you she vould like someting in de man-village!" Silvair growled angrily.

Kate sniffed, mopping at her eyes, trying to regain control. "It's not that! It's beautiful! I love it. I'm just ... so happy!" she wailed.

"She doan vant dis place," Sergei said emphatically. "She just doan vant to tell us she doan like it!"

Kate mastered her tears with an effort. "No. I really do like it! I liked it *before* I realized you'd bought for me," she said firmly, despite the wobble in her chin. "It's ... it was just such a wonderful surprise."

They studied her doubtfully when she started sobbing again.

"I stay and fix dis place up much better," Sergei said coaxingly.

Kate blinked her tears back, sniffing. "You will?" she asked, brightening immediately.

"I stay, too," Silvair growled, daring Sergei to exclude him. "I doan know vorking vid de vood, but I help Sergei it go faster, make better quicker."

Kate's smile wavered at that, but she kept it firmly in place. "We're going to all stay here together, then?"

Silvair and Sergei eyed one another with marked hostility.

"For now, I mean?" Kate added hastily. "I mean, we might as well. It'll save money not having to pay for a hotel and there's plenty of room for everyone to sleep."

Both men moved to the bedroom and studied the narrow bed.

Despite Kate's optimism, it took two days to get the power on, clean the place, which hadn't been lived in in several years, and replace the rotting mattress in the single bedroom the cabin boasted.

Neither man was terribly pleased about the sleeping arrangements, which thoroughly puzzled Kate since the three of them had been sleeping together ever since they'd been together. It wasn't really comfortable for any of them since Sergei and Silvair glared at each other balefully across her every night before they finally settled down to sleep.

Two days after they moved in and started working on refurbishing the cabin, Sergei and Silvair disappeared at dusk and returned several hours later so battered Kate was horrified. When she asked them what had happened, the two men merely scowled at one another evilly and refused to comment. Silvair slept on the couch that night, though.

The following week when they disappeared again, came back in a similar condition, and Sergei slept on the couch, she began suspect they weren't getting along at all well. It mystified her. They hadn't always seen eye to eye, and she'd gotten the impression many times that there was some one upmanship going on between them, particularly when it came to fucking her, but most of the time they seemed to be in accord. No matter what came up, they consulted with one another before they came to a decision.

She would've been more inclined to pursue the mystery if she hadn't made a discovery that wiped their antagonism from her mind.

She was pregnant. She tried very hard to convince herself she wasn't as soon as the idea popped into her head, but she'd never just 'missed' a period in her life and besides that, her belly was ballooning too fast to put it down to swelling.

Worse, she wasn't *just* pregnant. She knew she was a chip off the old block. Like her mother, she was blossoming with twins.   Nothing else could possibly explain such an unprecedented expansion of her waist and belly so quickly after conception because she knew without a doubt that only Silvair or Sergei could have fathered the babies. She hadn't been with anyone else for months before that and, in any case, she'd been on birth control.

It was the realization that she hadn't renewed on schedule, the missed period, and the fact that she couldn't fasten or zip her jeans anymore that added up to an impossible to dismiss realization.

She also couldn't convince herself it wasn't twins and that meant it wasn't going to be her little secret for very long. She hadn't gotten the chance to know her mother, and her grandparents had been very careful about the stories they passed to her about her mother, but no one else had worried about her overhearing unflattering tales about her mother.

If it had been only one, she might have been able to keep it a secret for months.

She felt like crying, another symptom of her condition that she'd been able to ignore—the desire to cry at the drop of a hat—not that she hadn't had plenty of provocation, but the pregnancy still explained why she'd had such a hard time controlling herself when she usually didn't.

She supposed the fact that she never seemed to feel as if she'd gotten enough sleep could also be attributed to her condition.

She'd grown hopeful that Sergei and Silvair might stay, at least for a while, even though she was beginning to have a very hard time coming up with something else that needed fixing.

Should she just confess, she wondered, and watch them take to their heels?

Or keep it to herself until it was so blatantly obvious even a man, who was predisposed to remain oblivious to this sort thing as long as possible, noticed?

By her reckoning, she was roughly two months pregnant when they began to stare at her belly with puzzlement. She managed to make it through another week before they confronted her and asked her point blank.

She'd just woken up, which made it worse, because she didn't have her wits about her.

"What's dis?" Sergei asked, stroking his hand slowly over her rounded belly, instantly alerting Kate to the fact that this was no prelude to sex.

"My belly," she muttered.

"Why is round?" Silvair demanded with just enough determination in his voice that she knew he'd already guessed, even if Sergei hadn't.

But then his mate, she recalled, had had a son for him.

She glared at him, knowing there was no point in lying. "Because I'm pregnant," she ground out baldly.

Contrary to what she'd expected, both men looked as if they'd been clobbered right between the eyes. For a split second after the stunned look left their faces, she could've sworn they looked pleased, but the moment passed too swiftly to be certain. They glared at one another furiously.

"Is mine?" Sergei demanded.

"Dis my baby?" Silvair demanded at almost the same moment.

She scowled at both of them, struggling with a fresh desire to weep. "How the hell would I know?" she demanded angrily. "You've both been fucking me! All I can say is they belong to one of you!"

She could only interpret the look they exchanged as horrified dismay. Fury descended over their faces in the next moment.

"Is mine, I stay!" Sergei growled.

"Is mine, I stay!" Silvair snarled back at him.

Anger had a way of depriving both of them of the ability to translate their thoughts into English, but Kate had no trouble interpreting the fury that was threatening to erupt between them. Grabbing her pillow, she smacked both of them in the head. "If you're going to fight about who has to stay, damn it, you can *both* leave!" she snarled at them when they turned to glare at her.

They went slack faced with stunned surprise. It held them until she'd scrambled out of the bed and stalked toward the bathroom.

"Nyet, Katie! Dis is wrong. Wrong tink. Katie, you tink wrong ting!" Sergei said a little desperately. "Is mine, I stay!"

Kate had stopped and turned when she realized he was trying to explain. At that last, however, she merely glared at him, stalked into the bathroom and slammed the door.

She was just working herself up for a really good cry when she heard the snarl that didn't sound like anything that would come from a human throat. The answering roar of the lion was unmistakable. Kate hesitated with her hand on the door knob for a handful of seconds, but as she heard all hell break loose in the bedroom, she retreated to shower and climbed in, cowering in the corner until silence finally fell in the room.

Terrified that she was going to find two broken, bleeding bodies in the other room, it took her a while to get up the nerve to unlock the bathroom door and peer out through a tiny crack at the room beyond. Relief filled her when she saw no sign of either man—or beast.

The room, however, was a shambles.

Heartened that they at least hadn't managed to kill each other, she moved through the room cautiously and peered into the living area. Seeing there was still no sign of either one, she crossed the room to look out the windows and then moved into the kitchen to look out.

Both men were standing in the yard, stark naked, washing the blood of their battles off with the water hose.

She watched them for several moments and finally opened the back door and went out. They spotted her immediately. Feeling weak kneed, Kate sat down on the back porch steps.

After studying her uneasily for several moments, Sergei dropped the hose he was holding and strode toward her purposefully. Crouching at her feet when he reached her, he looked up at her earnestly. "I luf you, Katie. I want to stay. Dis baby mine, it mean you feel de mating, too, understand?"

Kate felt her heart swell with tentative hopefulness. Tears filled her eyes. "I don't think I understand," she said finally, glancing at Silvair as he joined them. "You weren't fighting over who had to stay with me?"

Silvair frowned. "Is different vith man-child," he said. "Most time, no baby and den no true mating. Legend say if de voman of de man-child love de man-beast, den she give him baby, an' is true mating. Ve both claim you. Fight to see vhich of us is strongest, but dat doan vork vid you. You doan choose. So, ve know vhen de baby come. Is mine, den you choose me. Is his, den you are his woman."

Kate stared at him while that slowly sank in and created more chaos and distress instead of less. "But … it's always been the three of us! How can I choose one of you when I love both of you?"

Sergei and Silvair both stared at her for a long moment before they turned and looked at one another.

"Vhich you love more?" Silvair demanded after a prolonged silence.

Sergei stood up. "We see when de baby come. Is my baby, she is my woman. You go."

Silvair glared at him. "Is my baby, you go!"

Kate got up and went in the house and slammed the door.

* * * *

Contrary to what Kate had expected, Silvair and Sergei seemed satisfied they'd resolved the situation. The months of her pregnancy weren't completely peaceful, but, although they tended to blow up at one another from time to time, they were generally satisfied with just bellowing at one another in their native tongues.

Kate wasn't certain how that worked to resolve anything. Sergei couldn't speak or understand German. Silvair couldn't speak or understand Russian. She couldn't speak or understand either one, so she didn't actually know what they were saying to each other. It seemed to satisfy their need to act out their aggression toward one another, however.

Silvair opened a garage and began to spend more and more of his time repairing cars, which helped to ease the tension. Sergei, also running low on money since they'd both spent most of it on buying the car and the house, rented a small building and began to make furniture, creating pieces that were so exquisitely crafted people seemed to find it impossible to resist whatever the asking price.

Kate allowed them to talk her out of getting a job, mostly because she knew at the rate she was growing she wouldn't be able to keep it long.

As soon as they discovered she was carrying twins, Sergei and Silvair both took credit for it since they were equally convinced they were the father. She decided not to tell them she was hereditarily predisposed to have twins. They seemed to take such pride in their virility it didn't seem right to burst their bubble.

She didn't even consider the possibility that the babies might take after their father until she was nearing term. She might not have then except that Silvair disapproved the idea of having the babies in a hospital.

"Is natural. De babies come vhen dey are ready. Vhy you vant to have dem in dat kind of place?"

Kate frowned at him. "Do you know how to deliver a baby?"

His eyes widened. "No."

She studied him doubtfully for a moment as it occurred to her to wonder if there was a reason, besides the fact that he didn't like doctors or hospitals, why he didn't think she should. "Do you think they'll be born in their feline skin?"

He looked startled for a moment. "Conceive it in dis form—man-skin. Is born dis way." He was silent for a long moment. "Dis child part man-child. It may not be able to take de form of de father at all."

Kate was surprised at how dismayed she was about that. She should've been relieved but there was no getting around the fact that she wasn't and she finally realized it was because she loved Sergei and Silvair so much. She wanted the babies to be like their father. She was afraid he wouldn't feel like it was his if it wasn't like him.

There wasn't anything she could do about it, however.

"If that isn't something we need to worry about, then I'm having them in the hospital. It's twins. They might have special needs. They're usually smaller when a woman carries two than if there's only one."

"Is part man-beast. Dey be strong, very strong, even if leedle." He didn't argue the matter any further, though. In fact, he and Sergei became more and more anxious the closer she came to her time and changed their hours of working in their shops so that one of them was with her all the time. Kate had mixed feelings about that.

It was reassuring. It would be her first delivery and she was anxious herself so she was glad she didn't have to worry about going into labor when she was alone. It was also nice to have alone time with both of them even if she wasn't in any condition to actually enjoy it. On the bad side, the hovering got on her nerves and when she was with only Sergei, or only Silvair, it emphasized the fact that she was facing a time when it would be like that. Soon, she would have the babies and one of them would leave.

It didn't even matter if she decided she *did* love one of them more than the other. They'd made up their minds that whoever had fathered the twins would stay and the other would leave.

And she couldn't honestly say she did love one more than the other. She felt just as miserable when she thought about Sergei leaving as she did when she considered it might be Silvair.

It was unfair for them to expect her to choose, now, when it had been the three of them from the beginning. If she hadn't been with both of them, constantly, intimately, from the start, maybe she could've loved one more than the other, but it hadn't been that way and besides loving both of them, she was *used* to being with both of them. It seemed strange to think of it *not* being that way.

And very depressing.

She was in her eighth month when the cops finally tracked her down. She'd decided she wasn't going in to talk to them unless they did track her down, but she also wasn't going to try to hide. The idea of using an alias was just too unnerving even if she'd had some idea how to go about arranging such a thing.

She'd escaped Panas. She wasn't going to live under that kind of cloud anymore. They were the thugs, not her.

The clan, which Sergei and Silvair had both joined even though they lived a state away, helped them obtain the papers they needed to be 'legal' but the council didn't want to recognize her as a clan member when she was man-child, even if she was 'sort of' Sergei's and Silvair's mate. The clan council disapproved as much as the neighbors, so even though Sergei and Silvair were certain they could convince the council to accept her and help her with creating a new identity, she declined.

She didn't need anyone's approval but Sergei's and Silvair's and she meant to see that her babies didn't grow up feeling as if they had anything to be ashamed of. She was going to be completely straightforward about it and they would get the approval they needed at home and have the confidence they needed to ignore anyone who disapproved.

She could see as soon as the cops settled to questioning her that her distended belly made them extremely uneasy. They tried bullying her anyway, but their uneasiness made it possible for her to remain calm and she stuck to her story—as close to the absolute truth as she dared.

She'd gone back to the club because she was concerned about the great cats they were keeping caged there and arrived in time to be shot at by Panas' men. She had no first hand knowledge of anything that had happened in the club from the time she'd left. She'd fled the scene in fear for her life.

They weren't satisfied, but they couldn't think of anything to charge her with except leaving the scene of a crime and not coming forward with information and since they'd already 'solved' everything to suit themselves, they decided to let it go.

Her water broke, fortuitously, at about the time they were

trying to decide whether they wanted to be petty and find something to charge her with just for the aggravation of having spent so much time looking for her. Otherwise, they might have. As it was, they were just glad to tie everything up and get her out of the police station before they had more to clean up than amniotic fluid.

She might have been embarrassed except for the fact that she was in too much pain by that time to care if the sky fell. Sergei, who had accompanied her, drove her to the hospital. Outwardly, he appeared perfectly calm, but every time she groaned on a particularly hard pain, he ran off the edge of the road. After the second time he scared the shit out of her, she managed to focus on her breathing techniques.

Since he only stared at her blankly when she told him to go call Silvair once they reached the hospital, she ignored the nurses and used the pay phone to call him herself. Much to her dismay, she discovered there was no great rush. Despite the regularity of the contractions, it was six hours and thirteen minutes later before her first bouncing baby boy made his appearance. Five minutes later, the second arrived.

Sergei and Silvair, who'd had no interest at all in accompanying her into the delivery room, paced the waiting room and nearly came to blows twice during that time. When the duty nurse informed them she'd have them escorted off the premises if they didn't behave themselves, they growled at her, but settled to pacing and muttering instead of open hostility toward one another.

Kate, of course, knew nothing about it until later, but she wasn't the least surprised when the orderly in charge of her room informed her of it. By then, however, peace had been established.

Of a sort.

Kate might have been the second woman to make the Book of World Records if she'd been inclined to claim her spot. She wasn't. She was just thrilled beyond words to discover Sergei's and Silvair's diligence and determination had paid off. They were *both* present at the crucial moment when her two little eggs made their way down her fallopian tubes.

The moment the babies were wheeled out of the delivery room to be presented to the 'father', both men strode to the incubators and examined the infants thoroughly, specifically their scents. Grinning broadly, Sergei lifted his head and looked at Silvair. "Is mine."

"Dis mine," Silvair informed him, also grinning.

The information wiped the grins off of both faces, replacing them with scowls. After glaring at one another for a moment, they changed places and examined the other infant. By the time they'd tested both babies twice more, they were as puzzled as the nurse that had escorted the babies to the waiting room.

"Ms. Martin is in recovery. Uh ... whichever of you is the father can go in to see her."

Silvair and Sergei exchanged a furious look. "Is mine," they both said almost in unison, pointing to the baby they knew positively as their son.

The nurse gaped at them. "Just wait here for a minute. I'll speak with Ms. Martin," she said hurriedly, wheeling the incubators down to the nursery.

Kate, woozy from the pain medication she'd been given, stared at the woman in incomprehension when she bustled into the recovery room to ask which of the two 'gentlemen' in the waiting room was the father. "They didn't tell you?"

The woman pursed her lips disapprovingly. "They're both claiming the babies."

Kate blinked at her. "What?"

"*Each* of them is claiming he fathered *one* of the babies," the nurse clarified.

Kate gaped at her for a moment before a smile curled her lips. "I want to see *both* of them," she said firmly.

Clearly, the nurse disapproved, but she left. A few minutes later, Sergei and Silvair, both looking torn between elation, resentment, and confusion, entered the room cautiously. Kate smiled at them a little drunkenly. "They're beautiful, aren't they?"

Sergei strode to the bed and clasped her hand. "My son is beautiful," he said huskily, leaning down to kiss her.

She looked at him a little uncertainly when he straightened, but Silvair distracted her by leaning down to kiss her, as well. "My son is perfect," he informed her with a shaky grin.

Sergei glared at him when he straightened. "My son is beeg and strong and much more handsome dan yours."

Silvair scowled back at him. "Dat boy beeg ugly ting like his father."

"Now wait just a damned minute!" Kate snapped, glancing from one to the other with a mulish set to her jaw. "*My* sons are both beautiful!"

Silvair looked at her sheepishly. "Dey both beautiful like dere mudder. I just say dat 'cause he think de tiger more handsome wid his flashy pelt. You did goot, Katie, make two fine sons."

Mollified, Kate turned to look at Sergei expectantly. "Dey both fine, strong sons, Katie," he said almost reluctantly, then added, flicking a glare in Silvair's direction, "But mine is *more* handsome."

Kate sighed impatiently, but she felt giddy with the thought that she'd had one son for each of them. She plucked at the cover. "So—what happens now?"

They stared at her in puzzlement.

She shrugged. "You said one of you would leave."

Sergei and Silvair shared a look of hostility, but, after a moment, they both seemed to relax fractionally. "What do you want, Katie?" Sergei asked her.

Her chin wobbled, but she tamped the urge to cry. "If there's anything to the legend you told me about, doesn't it prove I love both of you when I had a baby for each of you? Doesn't that mean we're mated? That I'm *your* mate and yours?" she asked, looking from Sergei to Silvair.

"Felines doan form packs," Silvair said gently, if somewhat irritably.

"It's worked so far," Kate pointed out. "Don't you both want to be here to raise your sons?"

Sergei released an irritated breath. "Doan look like I got no choice but to stay. I luf you an' you have my son. I stay, Katie … if you want me to stay. Doan know how dis ting gonna work, but I want to stay wid you."

Relieved, Kate lifted her arms in invitation and hugged him tightly when he leaned down to kiss her. He flicked a glance at Silvair when he straightened. "I go look at dat handsome boy you give me."

She studied Silvair uncertainly when Sergei had left. Silvair shook his head. "I doan know no female—feline or man-child—anyting like you, Katie," he said finally, smiling faintly. "You know de male lion supposed to have de harem not de udder vay 'round? I guess if dat ol' tiger tink he can handle bein' part of dis strange pride, I can."

Kate clutched him tightly when he leaned down to kiss her. "It's your own fault, you know," she said shakily. "You made me fall in love with both of you."

He chuckled in spite of the irritation in his eyes. "Dat vas not de plan, Katie, but I can't say I'm sorry if de alternative vas not to have you. I luf you."

The End